Flight of the Maita
Book 12b
Palace Affair

Tab and TR are sent to a world in an early iron age to find who or what is interfering with the society there. Tab takes on the disguise of an alchemist and discovers the king's sorcerer is meeting aliens who are giving him technology.

Who? Why?.

<u>Critic comment</u>
I like this one. I still do not like the M-82nds.
– PA Rtng: More than worth the price

Contents

About the author

CD was born in Lakeland, Florida, in 1938. He is educated in genetics and botany. He has traveled over much of the world, particularly when he was in music as a rock rhythm guitarist with some well-known bands in the late sixties and early seventies. He has worked as a high steel worker and as a longshoreman, clerk, orchidist, bar owner, salvage yard manager and landscaper – among other things.

CD began writing fiction in 1984 and has more than 300 books published as of 3/15/16 in SciFi, murder, orchid culture and various other fields.

He now resides in Puerto Armuelles, David, and Gualaca, Chiriqui, Panamá, where he continues research into epiphytic plants and plays music with friends. He loves the culture of the indigenous people and counts a majority of his closer friends among that group. Several have "adopted" him as their father. He funds those he can afford through the universities where they have all excelled. "The Indios are very intelligent people, they are simply too poor (in material things and money. Culturally, they are very wealthy) to pursue higher education."

CD loves Panamá and the people, despite horrendous experiences (Free e-book; *Fading Paradise*). He plans to spend the rest of his life in the paradise that is Panamá

- Estrelita Suarez V. de Jaramillo – 3/15/2016

CD is involved in research of natural cancer cure at this time. It has proven effective in all cases, so far. It is based on a plant that has been in use for thousands of years, is safe, available, and cheap. He has studied botany, and was cured of a serious lymphoma with use of the plant, *Ambrosia peruviana*.

Information about this cure is free on the FaceBook group, Ambrosia peruviana for cancer. CD asks only that all who try it please report on its effectiveness on that group.

Palace Affair

Prologue

"Now what?" Tab mumbled as his ship, TRD-60, rushed him at InterDimensional mode TTH14 speed toward the planet, Neeahna, and the being known as Louahna.

Louahna was a being caught in two dimensional planes at once so she appeared as a fuzzy figure – which didn't much bother Tab. He was a robot, himself!

The emperor and its crew had been on the verge of aiding a new race and now Louahna comes along with one of her little problems.

Now!

As Tab was designed by the emperor to handle these kinds of problems he didn't really have an argument against going to Louahna's. He would never admit he enjoyed the weird kinds of things she came up with, but he did.

TR, the ship, was actually a part of Tab, but had a sep-arate personality of its own. Both TR and Tab were highly intelligent and the combination was awesome. They were programmed with an organic's reactions and thought patterns and had a very developed sense of humor. That was because one of the emperor's crew, the Terran, Z, had forced them all to develop the sense of humor or be doomed to never knowing what the hell was going on!

"TR?" Tab said.

"Yo!"

"What the hell does Louahna want now?" Tab asked.

"I haven't got the foggiest (Another thing from the Terran. Expressions that didn't make sense – but which the crew were all programmed to understand. TR liked to use them)," TR replied. "She got with Maita and told it what was on her mind. It was so private even Thing was left out."

Thing was a little tentacled empath who traveled with the emperor.

"That must have been one hell of a project!" Tab said. "How do you keep something from an empath?"

"You shield or ask it not to eavesdrop!" TR snapped. "We're now in TTH four for maybe the next ten minutes."

They landed on Neeahna, but Louahna wasn't there so they left for Neeneeahna where she might be. She sud-denly stepped through the wall into the pilot's dome. Being in two planes she could do that.

"Ready for some fun?" she asked.

"I hope!" TR replied. "It better be worth leaving the job we were on!"

"What've you got?" Tab asked.

"Remember how you and Z did that thing with the stocks on Hellrun?" she asked.

"I'm a machine. I don't forget," he answered. "And we both know that ain't true!"

"You don't forget you just fail to recall at a specific time or situation," she corrected. "I have a thing of the same general sort, but it's not a stock market thing. You'll have to come up with your own ideas, but the character you played there might be good for this."

"All the ass did was swear all the time!" TR snarled. "He was mostly obnoxious!"

"But lovable!" Tab quickly added.

"That's exactly what I mean," Louahna replied. "It might be just the thing considering what the queen's like.

"The world is called Klemmr and the people are much like the Swaz. You'll only have to get rid of the dorsal fin and webbing between the fingers and widen the crest. The gill slits have to go and you're metallic bronze instead of tan. They're in a stage of kings and castles so you can be the castle alchemist. They're pretty powerful and you can be obnoxious as part of the character.

"Something's wrong there. You'll have to find out what it is. It's possible they've found some new physical law and are working their magic off of it. The race could even-tually be a great one, but I think this is a crisis situation."

"Magic?" TR asked. "Z and Tom have all the experience with that. Thing, too. Why not get them? Tom would love a little adventure now that he's raised his family."

"Zianteus was the magician on Tlorg," she explained. "We were in control. This one is very different. It's some-thing I happened to come across while I was studying some plants. I don't have the time to spend there and the world's not my project. It seems to be something that could lead to a very bad situation in a few hundred years, but can probably be corrected easily now. These things usually aren't serious if caught early. I worry there could be outside influence, but it's indefinite enough that it should be investigated. If it's a new physical law we must learn it and be able to study it. If it's outside interference it must be stopped!"

"Give me the coordinates and I'll see what I can do," Tab said. "You might tell me what I'm to do with TR."

"TR will have to orbit," she answered. "You can disguise a floater somehow and it can be there in that form. There are lots of forests so you can go in anytime. There are some bandits and highwaymen. It's that era.

"The planet's at W one thirty five, plus two, N oh seventy six sixteen. The city's at grid lat oh twenty nine point four lon one seventy six point fourteen. That seems to be the main seat of the trouble. It's most fortunate that it's a relatively small keep. A small town built around a castle.

"Good luck!"

She stepped through the wall and was gone and, as usual with her, Tab wouldn't have any idea what he was looking for when he got there.

They were over the planet. It was a verdant place with a lot of oceans and island nations. Louahna had given TR a general sketch of the best area for their investigations, a town on a river with a large stone castle and a large enough population to where they would be able to make changes that would spread over time while small enough that an investigation would uncover all there was to know about the place.

TR used a variety of highly sensitive sensor scanners that located everything in the immediate area after a short time.

"Hey, Boss?" TR asked.

"Yo!" Tab replied.

"There's lots of deep water near your base. Why don't I stay down there?"

"It's okay with me," Tab said. "There are a lot of ships so you might come in handy as the only submarine on the world. Sit down near the mouth of the river and I'll go up it on the floater to the forest upstream tonight and walk back to the town tomorrow morning at dawnlight.

"Give me the smallest retracting floater you can and I'll wrap it like one of the big hats they wear. It has to have a lot of things built in. I'll get into the medbox so you can modify me to what the floater scans say. You can get the language with a probe while somebody's asleep.

"They don't have much in the way of advanced tech-nology so I won't have to be shielded against scanners or that kind of stuff, but I'll need a deflector shield to stop projectiles. It would be unfortunate to be shielded against beams and lasers then to have a spear break something!"

"I'll make the floater into a shield," TR replied. "Lots of these people carry them and you can hang it on the wall or something. I'll put in all the shields and small weapons as well as com relays and a larger powerpack. You'll need that to boost through the water, but maybe I can put a small antenna on a float in a bunch of seaweed or some-thing. I'll be too deep to find, which ain't deep here."

"Input all you have about their weapons and armaments for me," Tab suggested.

"What for? We'll be in contact. I can send," TR replied.

"All you have about their magic, too," Tab continued. "I may need it fast and I have more than enough capacity to carry it onboard."

They made the few modifications on Tab after TR went under the ocean far out, then approached beneath the surface. Tab took the floater soon after dark to make his way cautiously up the river to where he was upstream from the town. He waited near the road until the sun was up. He was plodding toward the town, about a kilometer away, when he met a band of highwaymen. The floater had a mind probe and other sensors on it which Tab must use. He had to get a native into the headgear to have the local dialect and for TR to analyze the exact racial odor (One of the most important parts of any disguise) so this was really a fortunate thing. He'd hoped to find a subject before daylight, but none traveled the road in the dark hours.

There were seven in the band who surrounded him with swords, clubs, and knives. They made sounds obviously demanding his valuables. From the look of them they would kill him with or without his cooperation so he had the floater anesthetize them all, then put the probe on the leader. He took their weapons, which he sent on the floater back to TR who processed the language and customs for the crystal and sent it back on the floater, which then contracted to again become his shield. It met him a few meters outside the gates to the town where he placed the racial odor generator and the crystal that contained the language, customs and habits of the people.

He then approached the gate. The guards looked him over, but didn't stop him.

Inside the walls the town was dirty and drab. There were several inns and pubs along a narrow, dark, wet, dingy path that led to the castle.

He walked amid stares to near the castle gates where he entered a pub, ordered a sort of beer and bread and asked the latest news.

The pub was neat and clean inside.

The language gave him the customs and manners of the subject probed, but also gave the subject's knowledge of the ways of the higher classes. The bandit probed was once a page for a duke and duchess so had been exposed to the ways of the elite. The mind stores everything it observes even when the person isn't aware the material's there, so to speak.

The pub owner came to silently stand near the table when the waitress left after serving the food, some quarter of an hour later.

"Is there something you wish?" Tab asked. He knew from the crystal it was bad form for a person in service to ask questions of the higher classes unless invited to do so.

"You seem an outlander," the man replied. "You came from the main gates along river road.

"There were seven bodies found in a heap a short dis-tance away. Did you pass them?"

Tab considered for a moment and came to a conclusion. "Do you mean the bandits?" he asked.

"I didn't ever suggest that they were bandits," the proprietor answered. "They carried no weapons and the guard found the bodies without marks on them so feel it might be a sorcerer's spell."

He was speaking with great difficulty and was choosing his

words carefully so Tab decided to put him at ease.

"I'm the alchemist, Northram, from the North Country," he said in a friendly tone. "If I am taken to the bodies I'll resurrect them and we'll see if they are in fact bandits. It wasn't done through sorcery, but through science."

The anesthetic the floater used would place the Klemmr in a comatose state much like death, TR sent, then Tab's internal communications a few moments later told him a strong antidote might be required for the Klemmr phy-siology. It was in a vial in the medical supplies.

This was a stroke of luck – if the bandits hadn't been disposed of yet. He could appear to be a very powerful alchemist indeed!

"I'm called Wooler," the man answered. "I'll see if the bodies are still unburied, Sir Northram."

Tab nodded and finished the breakfast. Two palace guards came in and spoke to Wooler for a moment, then came to him.

"Up, you!" one of them demanded.

"Drop dead!" Tab snarled in reply. "And don't think for one moment I say that idly! Look at those seven bandits and think before you start any crap with me!"

The guard grabbed at his shoulder and he sent a heavy charge through his metallic skin. The guard was thrown against the wall where he lay senseless.

Tab turned to the second guard and said, "He'll recover – this time! I assume you want to take me to the bandits. I'm prepared to accompany you, but don't be fool enough to try any of that crap, ordering me around. It won't work."

The guard was staring at his captain laying unconscious against the wall and swallowed hard. "He's only s'posed to make you come back to the gate to be 'dentified," he said.

"Fine! Then let's go to the gate," Tab said. He stood and placed a gold nugget on the table. "I really should've been stopped for identification as I entered the town. Perhaps we'll set a system here where we'll know who's in town at all times. It'll put a quick stop to a lot of the thievery so conveniently blamed on travelers if you can show there were no travelers here at the time, don't you think? It'd be an excellent way to root out the criminals in your midst.

"Come! Come! Shall we go to the gate?"

The guard seemed undecided as to whether he should help the captain or go along with Tab. The second choice prevailed and he came out asking, "What'd you do to Greak?"

"I only shocked him a bit. He needed the lesson, I think," Tab answered. "I'm called Northram. What's your name?"

The guard fidgeted, so Tab said, "I'm not a sorcerer. I'm an alchemist."

"Uh, my name's Estridge," the guard answered.

"Tell me about the bandits," Tab said.

"You mean the dead men?" Estridge asked. "Thed, Funt, 'n Mo found 'em in a heap on the road comin' in. I don't think they's any highwaymen cause they didn't have no weapons.

"They's a lot of 'em 'tween towns round here. Lots 'a people gits robbed er worse, but we can't charge 'em with nothin' ef they ain't got no weapons. Court'll jest say you ain't no bandit ef ya ain't got no weapon!"

"I've turned their weapons to straw and rocks," Tab replied. "Straw blew away in the wind."

"But you done sed as you ain't no sorcerer!" Estridge cried. "A sorcerer turns one thing inna another!"

"No," Tab said, wishing he would think before saying things. "A sorcerer uses magic to trick you into believing he's changed things. An alchemist does what we call trans-mutations of things, which doesn't really change much. Straw is material from small plants and the wood of their spears is material from larger plants. I merely transmuted it from one form to another of the same thing."

"Ah? An the swords and spearheads?" Estridge asked suspiciously. "*They* ain't no plant stuff!"

"The bronze is metal melted from rocks," Tab replied. "If you check in the area where you found the bandits you'll find I've transmuted the metal *back* into the rocks."

He called TR on the internals and said to get some copper and other ores into the area in case they checked.

"Take me to the bodies now I'll resurrect them and you may question them as to whether they're bandits."

"It don't make no differnce," Estridge said. "They wasn't in no city."

"You mean to tell me this city doesn't protect travelers on its roads?" Tab asked. "That isn't acceptable! The people are taxed and they must be protected! I'll see to it!"

"I hope you can, but you ain't gonna make the king 'n queen do nothin' what they don't wanna do!" Estridge replied. "The bodies is in here. The captain was gonna find out who you were so's if they's got kin what want to bring a gree, er, a what'd'ya call it."

"A grievance," Tab said. "I might bring a grievance against them after I bring them back to life."

Only five of the bandits were there. "Where are the other two?" he asked. "There were seven."

"They done been buried," Estridge said. "They's diggin' holes fer these out'n back now. The healer says it ain't smart to leave 'em layin' round fer the vultures 'cause WE could get sick. I seen that b'fore. They stink after awhile, too."

"How true," Tab agreed and made a pass over the faces of each of the five comatose bandits laying there as he surreptitiously injected them with the antidote with the other hand and they began to stir, then sat up less than a minute later.

"Whoa! I thought you'd done sed you ain't no sorcerer!" Estridge shouted as two more guards came in the door and stood staring wide-eyed at the five "dead" bandits sitting there shaking their heads and gibbering.

"I'm not," Tab insisted. "I'm a scientist. An alchemist."

"Where's Greak?" one of the guards asked. "How'd he do that? They was *dead*!"

"No. They weren't dead. They were merely in suspended animation," Tab corrected. "They attacked me so I taught them a lesson."

"You mean the two we done buried ain't dead?" he asked.

"They will be by now," Tab replied. "I really should've left these others dead except for the one I may want to question, but I've always been softhearted."

Estridge shot him a quick grin.

"You!" Tab snapped at the bandit leader.

"Huh? Wha? Me?" the bandit muttered.

"How long have you been robbing people along that road?" he asked.

He had the crystal of this one's mind and knew the man was raised as a bandit, as were the rest of the gang. They were the group responsible for a number of deaths, rapes and a large number of robberies along River Road. It was considered their territory by other bandit bands.

"What're you talkin' about!?" the bandit cried. "I ain't no highwayman!"

"Oh? Did you like being dead?" Tab asked. "You'll ans-wer my questions – and honestly – or I'll kill you again. Next time you stay dead!"

The bandit shook his head and stared at the floor. "I got to make a livin' same's anybody else!" he pleaded.

"Just answer my questions!" Tab instructed.

"Since I was just a sprout," the bandit muttered.

"How many have you killed?" Tab asked.

"I doan know! Lots!" the bandit replied.

"How many women have you raped?" Tab asked.

"I doan remember. Lots," he answered.

"And the rest of this scum with you?" Tab asked.

"We's family! We does things together!" the bandit ans-wered. "Where's Ollie and Hik?"

"They been buried," Estridge said. "They was buried 'fore we found he could bring 'em back."

"We gonna git you fer this!" the bandit snarled.

"I think the whole bunch of scum should be beheaded," Tab suggested. "They've admitted to murder and rape. Have any of *you* lost any relatives or friends along River Road?"

"Yuh! My sister was gang-raped along there!" Estridge cried.

"They did it then," Tab said. "River Road's their personal ter-ritory and nobody else works along it. That's why the city must protect those who pay the taxes."

"Hey!" the bandit leader yelled. "We pays our texes! We pay ever sarg 'a tha texes, same's everbody!"

"Are you saying the king and queen know you're high-waymen and they charge you taxes?" Tab asked.

"Sure!" the bandit replied. "We doan pay we doan work no more!"

"Then you guards had better protect your own families!" Tab snapped. "I always understood that's what a king and queen were for! Not to be part of the bandits themselves!"

Estridge was muttering with the other guards as Tab stalked out of the room. He heard the screams, but kept walking back toward the castle. He went back into the pub and ordered another liter of the sour beer and some more bread. The captain was still sitting at a table with his head in his hands.

"If you ever put your hands on me again you'll get a lot worse than a headache," Tab greeted as he walked by.

A half hour later Estridge came into the pub and went to the captain to ask, "Are you all right, Captain Greak?"

"Yeah! What happened?" Greak answered.

"You done made the mistake 'a grabbin' a alchemist," Estridge answered. "I ast 'im to come to the station and he give us I.D. He's legit."

"What about those dead 'uns?" Greak asked.

Estridge winked at Tab. "We already done buried 'em," he said. "They was startin' to stink. They was the type stunk real bad."

Estridge helped Greak to his feet and they started to walk out, first stopping at Tab's table.

"I ain't gonna grab at you no more," Greak promised. "I ain't stupid! I jus' want ya to know I ain't got no hard feelin's. I ast for it."

Tab reached into his robe pocket and took out a strong pain killer to hand to Greak. He wasn't sure how it would react on Greak's system, but it couldn't do any lasting harm. It might intoxicate him.

"Wooler!" he requested. "Bring the captain a cup of water, if you please.

"Take the powder with a little water and the headache will be gone in minutes. I like an intelligent man!

"Be careful the powder doesn't get you drunk.

"I believe I'll stroll over to the castle to see if they need an alchemist. I can turn lead into gold and can make medicines for the healer and all that kind of crap. What I hear about this king and queen tells me they'll really go for the gold bit.

"Have a seat for a minute and tell me what I should know about the king and queen."

Greak sat and took the powder with the water Wooler brought, so Tab told Wooler and Estridge to sit, too. There wasn't any other business so they could get to know one another.

"Well, King Lopar's mebbe a little bit hard," Greak explained. "He's got a lot 'a problems. People don't like 'im too much, but they ain't sayin' nothin' agin 'im. It doan pay good – an sides, it ain't him what's tha problem 'n people knows it.

"Queen Keenu's from Poosta – Kopett's daughter – so she makes 'er own deals onna side, 'f'n ya knows where the stream flows. Kopett ain't exakly royalty er nothin' like that. She's jest got alla that land onna border 'tween here 'n Poosta. Sorta what ya calls a buffer. Got another brat married Fripp over to Kwest. Meemi's 'er name. Lopar's been tryin' ta git in Meemi's bed-chamber's why he done married Keenu. Fripp wants a roll with Keenu so they sorta comes an goes an we ain't got to fight no border wars er nothin' so long's it stays like it is. We doan gripe much, but we git tired'a all tha crap we gotta put up with. Thas why I grabbed you.

"Wha's da stuff ya gimme? I'll buy all ya got! Whoa!

"All'a Kopetts kids got thosh big assh's'n wiggles 'em alla time. I'd liketa....

"Wha's da schtuff ya gimme?"

"It does makes you a bit drunk, but you have to admit! The headache's gone!" Tab replied.

"Whoo! Ya can shay ... say tha' agin! I ain' neber felt thish good!"

Estridge grinned, winked at Tab, shook his head and helped Greak to his feet and they staggered out of the pub.

"I thought you was gonna resurrect those bandits," Wooler said.

"I did," Tab replied. "They were all right when I left. Of course, they had admitted to raping some of the guards' sisters and to murdering brothers and cousins and such so they might have had a sudden relapse, especially since they admitted they paid your wonderful king and queen to be allowed to work the River Road territory without inter-ference."

"They's bandits all over everywhere!" Wooler cried. "That's why nobody goes nowhere much!"

"Wooler, there's what we alchemists call a `scam' going on here," Tab explained. "The way it works is if someone in high places, such as Keenu and Lopar, allow bandits to do as they please so long as they get part of the loot for themselves. They can use the highwaymen to get rid of people they don't like and to keep people, as you say, from traveling much.

"When people travel they can get ideas – like they can throw people in high places in their own dungeons if they'll stick together and don't act too quickly. Premature action is disaster because you must first undercut the soldiers.

"If you'll just remember those soldiers out there have lost family and friends to these bandits you'll see they would join you in a movement by the townspeople to be rid of such things. It's all done with payoffs. The bandits give part of what they steal to Lopar and Keenu who in turn see the bandits are safe and they get wealthy people on the road now and then.

"Your leaders do send wealthy people they don't like much out on errands from which they never return, don't they?"

"Yuh! I allus though those bandits was payin' somebody off!" Wooler declared. "They get away with way too much! And they get away too easy!

"Are Lopar and Keenu really in it?

"I'd believe Keenu, but Lopar, too? I don't think...."

"Her up past her big wiggly ass and him up to his ugly neck!" Tab snapped. "I might be able to do something about it. I'm going to get a job at the castle, I think.

"Yeah, I just might do that. It'll be fun! I'm too powerful for them to fight. You might be wisest to forget I ever said a word in your presence, too."

"Hey! I'm deaf! I ain't heard nothin'!" Wooler cried. "Maybe you'd best check more on that bunch at the castle 'fore you do nothin' real permanent. I think Keenu's the real problem'n Lopar's too weak'n goes along. I seen times he don't seem, you know, to, how you say? – exakly approve 'a her doin's.

"Honest up. I don't think Lopar's the one. It's Keenu and maybe that advisor 'r whatever."

"Thanks. I'll bear that in mind," Tab promised. "We might have a little fun with this one. How'd you like to become Duke Wooler, caterer to the royal palace?"

"Are you jokin'?" Wooler asked.

"Hells, no!" Tab said. "I'm going to have some fun here and you might as well have some, too.

"Yes! I think I'm going to enjoy this! I'll see you later, Wooler. I'm going to call on the good king and queen!"

He put another gold nugget on the table. "Hey!" Wooler said. "You done already gimme enough to buy a new inn!"

"I can make all I want," Tab replied. "I could bury this town under ten meters of gold if I want.

"We're going to have some fun, Wooler. Oh, yes! We're going to have some fun!"

Tab stopped at the castle gates where two of the guards dropped their spears across his path. He pointed to the spears as the cutting laser on the floater cleanly sliced the shafts a few centimeters from their hands. They stared wide-eyed at the pieces laying at their feet.

"It's really very rude to place a weapon in the path of an innocent citizen," Tab confided. "A good butler should take the visitor's calling card and present it to the person or persons with whomever the caller wishes to converse."

"Hey! How'd you do that?" the guards yelled. The loud voices brought two more guards at a trot. They drew their swords and Tab chanted, "Microwave boogey-woogey with a hotsy totsy floy-floy!"

The two approaching guards felt their swords growing very hot and dropped them where they lay on the stones and smoked. The leather hides wrapped around the grips steamed and soon burst into flames. All the metal accou-trements, such as belt buckles, buttons, clasps, rings and coins in their pockets were getting hot, as well as their armor and helmets. Everything made of metal in a circle of two or so meters of them was getting uncomfortably warm.

"How very rude!" Tab cried. "You'd think someone around here would teach the hired help proper manners!"

Tab stopped the microwave bombardment from the floater before anyone was actually burned, but the guards were jumping around shedding articles of clothing in a frenzy. The commotion brought more guards as well as a few servants out, but a look from Tab was enough that no one else dared threaten him with a weapon.

"I suppose I'll just have to show *myself* around, now!" Tab remarked and smiled at the people gawking at him.

Tab approached a giggling girl in flowing robes and said, "I suppose your Queen Keenu and King Lopar are still busy in their bedchambers with whoever's sharing the quarters? I suppose it would be asking too much that they be up and around this early. The sun's only been up four hours.

"Would you kindly tell them the alchemist, Northram, is calling and would like to discuss employment in this horrendous pile of rocks they call a home, fair – and I might add, beautiful – maiden?"

The girl giggled again so he continued, "I can wait here for your return or I can come inside that atrocious excuse for a castle and await them. Whatever is most convenient for you, my lovely fair maiden."

She giggled again and said, "Lopar's up, but Keenu is still in her bed. I'll tell him you are here, Sir Northram, but I do not believe he will grant you audience."

"Take this to him then," Tab replied, handing her a large nugget that was gold on one side and lead on the other. "I'll turn the other half into gold for him at our meeting. Should that be denied you can bring the nugget back."

"He'll just keep it," she replied.

"In that eventuality I'll come looking for him," Tab returned with his smile.

She giggled again and went into the castle. Half an hour later she hadn't reappeared and the guard was milling about nervously, muttering. They refused to speak to him and were obviously afraid he'd go into the castle. They weren't at all confident they could stop him after his earlier demonstration.

He said, "Time's up!" and went to the door. The guards stood in front of it, barring his way.

"I think you've been warned enough about trying to stop me," he said loudly. "I'm going to get rough if you con-tinue in this stupidity. You *can't* stop me!"

The largest of the guards stepped toward him and snarled, "Oh, yeah? Well, I ain't fallin' for none of that magician crap! You go through that door through me or you don't go through that door – and you ain't big enough!"

Tab snapped a punch at the guard's jaw and had the floater anesthetize him at the same moment. The guard dropped.

"I'll resurrect him when I come back out," Tab said. "If any of you want to die stand there and I'll kill you. If anything happens to me in there I won't be back out to resurrect you. Think about it!"

He went to the door. The guards parted to let him through.

"If one of you will be so kind as to guide me I won't have to search through this oversized stone box looking in all the rooms myself," he said at the door.

A page stepped forward and pointed to a large carved door ahead. "Lopar's in there, but I ain't said nothin'!" he cried.

"Fair enough," Tab said. "I think I'll try that large carved door since you won't say."

He went toward the massive door where two very frightened guards crossed spears in front of him.

"There's a steel drop-bar inside the door," the floater's radio informed him on his internals. "I got an X-ray of it.

"Where do you suppose they got steel? They're hardly into iron."

"Laser the bar and hinges so the door will fall," he sent back. He held the "shield" in front of himself and the guards' spears fell into pieces. They backed against the wall and stood frozen.

The massive door creaked once, slowly leaned outward, then fell to within a few centimeters of his toes with a loud crash.

"You judged that a bit close, didn't you?" TR asked on the internals. Tab could feel the mirth in it. He'd always wondered how TR could get those kinds of things into an electronic voice – and on internals, yet!

"You *could* have had the damned door fall inward!" he sent back.

He looked to the two guards cowering to the side.

"Please remove this garbage from my path," he said to them. "Just lean it against the wall. I'm sure King Low Pants will want it replaced. It keeps the riffraff out!"

One of the guards caught on and grinned at him. He waved for the other and they dragged the heavy door to one side.

"Shield up!" came through the internals.

He raised the shield and stepped into the room where Lopar fired a heat laser at him from a scepter he was carrying.

"Microwave-a-boo-boo the staffy-waffy!" Tab ordered, then said to Lopar, "That's not a very nice way to greet an alchemist who sent you a gold calling card!"

The scepter popped, melted on the outer end and dripped to the floor with the stink of hot plastic. Lopar stared at him with his mouth hanging open, clamped his jaws shut, then showed anger.

"That was a magic wand! You've ruined it! Who are you?" he demanded.

"That was a scientific thingamajig I melted with another kind of whatzit and I'm Northram. Sir Northram to you," Tab replied evenly. "I'm an alchemist. I don't deal with magic, so your magician who made the staff for you is powerless against me.

"I only want a job doing those simple things like turning base metals into gold and have been treated rudely here. It is unconscionable! I very seldom allow myself to become this angered, but you're pushing my patience beyond the bonds of reason!

"Beware! Do not challenge my science! All of your magic is as that wand and will bring you destruction if you persist with this idiotic attack on me. You anger Sir Northram at your peril!"

He pointed to a large cut glass chandelier set with hundreds of smoky candles. It was held by a heavy steel chain. The chain parted and the chandelier crashed to the floor.

"How did you do that?!" Lopar cried. "Feltron can do it! He says it's magic!"

"Magic is merely unexplained science," Tab snapped. "I didn't come here to argue magic. I came here to seek employment. If you make it necessary I'll simply take over this place and boot you and your queen out on your stupid asses. Considering the way I've been treated thus far you don't deserve better.

"I intend to start giving certain strict orders around here starting right now. You'll see they're carried out or you'll end up washing the streets – with your tongues!

"The payoff from bandits and highwaymen will stop as of now! The guard will clean the area of that kind of scum.

"Have someone show me to my rooms – and they'd better be the best you have. I'll want a hot bath daily before retiring and will also oversee my own food prepar-ation until the cook knows what dishes I particularly like and how I like them. Don't bother trying to poison me. It won't work. I have immunity from such silliness. You don't.

"Have a few tons of lead brought to my quarters. I'll want

everything made out of gold. I'll also make a large vessel filled with jewels of all kinds. My cape will be the finest pure gold thread worked into plush green handspun crovin cloth, as will all the cloth used in my quarters.

"I think I look very good in green, don't you?

"Green and gold will be my colors! I'll need thousands of emeralds!"

"Hey!" Lopar cried. "We've only got the two emeralds and they belong to Keenu!"

"Oh, I make my own stuff," Tab replied offhandedly. "Don't you think rubies will be a great contrast to the emeralds? I can line everything in diamonds to set the colors off.

"Well? Where's a page to show me to my quarters? I don't have any intention to stand here all day!"

Not knowing what to do and fearing this Sir Northram, Lopar clapped his hands for the page to come to receive his instructions. When Tab walked out behind the page, Lopar stood staring, lost in utter confusion at the open space left by the missing door.

The page led Tab up to a tower with a large chamber on top, two rooms on two floors on the way upward and a stairway that led downward. Tab was prepared to befriend the page, but remembered the bandit leader was a page in his youth. It was possible Lopar was using the pages as a training school for thieves, killers, and worse so he remained quiet.

When the page left Tab radioed TR to have gold and jewels and fine cloth delivered by floater. TR could manufacture the things and have floaters bring it all after dark through the upper tower windows, which were barred. They would cut the bars and reweld them after the deliveries. If Lopar actually brought any lead in they could replace it with gold TR's floaters would extract from any number of places.

TR sent scanning floaters out to locate anything they might

need. Maita had designed and built TR's atomic architect machine that would build perfect gems, one atom at a time.

"There's an observation device in this room, one in each of the other rooms we passed through and various odd listening devices around," the floater reported.

"I detected them," Tab replied. "It's rather high-tech for this place wouldn't you say?"

"There's definitely some interference with this culture," TR sent. "Those devices aren't to be invented here for between one and two thousand years."

"I felt that from the first," Tab returned. "That laser in the wand Lopar used clinched it. I can't wait to meet this Feltron character. I suppose they think I can be locked away in this tower so I'll treat that as a joke. They'll have to meet me face-to-face with their hot-shot magician."

He inspected the room and found the best route for the tug floaters to use in delivering the valuables to him. The base of his tower was in the river so it should be easy enough, but he'd have to blind the observer sensors. If they weren't infra-red sensitive it would be easy.

He went down the stairs to inspect the rooms below and to the room through which he entered the tower. The steps downward led to a room below water level that was flooded.

"I'll bet they can drain that in almost no time," he sent to TR.

He considered going into the room to see where it led, but that would give away the fact he didn't need air so he went back up to the ground floor room. The door was barred closed on the outside as he expected so he used a pencil laser concealed in his sleeve to cut the iron bar, then strolled casually into the room where he'd left Lopar. There was a female with the king, who joined him in staring with wide-eyed disbelief as Tab strolled carelessly into the room.

"Ah! Queen Hiccup?" Tab asked as he approached them, "I

don't believe we've been introduced yet. I'm Sir Northram, alchemist extraordinaire! Lead into gold and all that kind of childish crap."

She drew herself up haughtily and stared down her nose at him, snapping, "I am called `Your Majesty' and I'm called *Queen Keenu!*"

"Hmm. I knew it was something like that," Tab replied pleasantly. "The tower was filthy, but it'll do nicely. I've cleaned it up. You really shouldn't live among the filth around here. It can be bad for the health. I mean, all that garbage thrown about – not just the type of people you associate with.

"Where will I find my personal cook, Queenie? I'll want to instruct her or him in how to prepare certain dishes. I'll supply the basic materials and spices.

"I certainly hope the dining areas are cleaner than this pfim stye here! You really should clean this place! Just because you were raised in a cesspool is no reason to have others live the same way. Really! I will never understand how you could get to be queen and never learn anything at all about the proper way to treat a guest.

"Oh, yes! There'll definitely have to be changes made around here.

"Definitely!

"No question at all!

"Positively!"

Lopar was sputtering and Keenu was about to explode. "How *dare* you!" she screamed. "How *dare* you to address *me* in such a manner! Queenie, in*deed*! I should have you beheaded!"

"Oh! That reminds me!" Tab said brightly. "I killed one of your guards on the way in and promised to resurrect him when I was settled in. Where will I find the body?"

Lopar's curiosity overcame his indignation. "Can you really bring him back to life?" he asked.

"Yes, certainly," Tab said. "Take me to him and I'll fix him up good as new – which wasn't all that good, in his case."

"Are you both mad?!" Keenu screamed.

"Oh, do sit down and shut up!" Tab snapped. "You give me a headache.

"The guard?"

Lopar clapped his hands and a page came to lead them to a room by the entrance where the guard was laid out on a table. Keenu's curiosity overcame her blind fury enough to where she tagged along. Tab went to the guard's "body" and made the pass over his face while injecting the anti-dote with the other hand. He then turned to go toward the door.

"Wait!" Lopar cried. "Why didn't it work?"

Tab turned and said, "Sit up you silly damned fool! They think you're still dead and will be burying you!"

The guard sat bolt upright and stared around, saying, "What happened?"

"You done been dead fer the last coupla hours's what! You was DEAD!" another guard said.

"I'm so cold!" the resurrected guard moaned.

"Your body temperature's down from being dead," Tab explained. "Wrap up in something until it's back up to normal."

He turned and walked out while Lopar asked the guard what it was like being dead.

"Cold and black!" the guard wailed. "So cold! Black! I don't know! I don't want no more of it!

"Cold and black!

"So black!

"So cold!"

Tab went back to the throne room, preceded by Keenu. She was now being attended by four females, one of whom was the girl who brought the gold nugget to Lopar from the courtyard earlier. She winked at him and he grinned in reply.

"Low Pants is questioning the guard," Tab said. "Where's my cook? I want to get started on preparing supper."

Keenu stared at him a moment, then resignedly nodded toward the girl nearest him, who was the one from the courtyard. She led him into a hallway where she said, "What did you do to Keenu? I've never seen her so en-raged about anything before!

"Oh! My name is Lolu. I'm her niece, Sir Northram."

"Just call me NN – Northram from the north," Tab answered. "The only ones who have to call me `Sir' are King Low Pants and Queen Hiccup and classless clods like them. I called her `Queenie' and `Hiccup.' She seemed to take some kind of offense. Strange."

Lolu giggled again and introduced him to a large, jolly woman. "This is Mima," Lolu said. "She's head cook and housekeeper and will assign someone to you."

"I done been listnin' through tha watcher hole, Lolu," Mima said. "Anybody'd cut ol' Keenu down what he done I cooks fer meself! I kin promise thet ya'll have a clean seat, too, an a clean table an clean service. I gonna put a girl jest ta keep yer rooms clean an proper, too. Thet scut oot thir dunt know if'n tha palace's clean er if'n it's tha pfim stye you done called ut – so I dunt clean ut!"

"I like you," Tab said. "You call me NN, Mima.

"I'll get some food and show you how I want it. The people who work here in the kitchen can eat what they want so long as I have what I want. I'll bring my own utensils and plates.

"Do all those people dine together?"

"They's usual fifteen er twenny fer a meal," Mima replied.

"Good!" Tab exclaimed. "I'll have a cleaner place and much better food than any of them. I'll eat from solid gold plates with knives and forks an spoons of a metal we alchemists call `chrome steel' set with jewels. The goblets and bowls will be the finest cut crystal glass in red, set with emeralds. I'll have a placemat of the finest spun-gold thread.

"We're going to have fun here!"

"But where will you get all that gold and jewelry?" Lolu asked cocking her head to the side to study him.

"I can make whatever I want," Tab answered. "Are you unattached?"

Lolu giggled and said, "Why, yes, Kind Sir!"

"Ah! You will show me the honor and kindness of accompanying me to meals and social functions, I pray?" Tab asked with his most charming smile.

"Why, I will be most honored, Kind Sir!" she replied with a giggle.

"I'll want you to have the finest of clothing and a lot of gold and jewelry," Tab continued. "We're going to have some fun people!

"Mima, you'll have to wear fine furs and a large tiara with matching necklace in gold, pearls and emeralds to show you're my personal chef."

"Oh, NN, Sir!" Mima exclaimed. "I ain't got no gold er fancy jewels!"

"Mima, you'll have so much gold and jewels tonight you can't carry them all!" Tab said with a laugh. "I'll want a warm bath each evening too so you can arrange for someone to handle that.

"I'm an alchemist. I invent things. I'm going to show you how to have what we alchemists call a 'shower'. The water will be carried to the top of my tower every morning where I'll make a thing to cause the sun to heat the water.

"I'll also show you how you can make the fat you render in cooking into a much better soap than anyone has by mixing in certain ashes and adding fine spices for scent for me and flower petals for the ladies.

"There'll be plenty of all this stuff for you and Lolu.

"I'll ask Lolu to please get your measurements so the fine clothes can be formed to fit you perfectly. When you have the measurements, please bring them to me in my tower, Lolu. I'll get your measurements then!"

"I will bring them soon," Lolu answered with a giggle.

Tab went to the tower room, put his shield on the listening device in the wall with enough force to destroy it, then had the tug floater remove the steel bars from the window for the carrier floaters. He called TR to send two large floaters with forming instructions and the cloth and to deliver a good many jewels and his and Lolu's place settings along with the serving trays and so forth. TR was in constant touch through the internals and devices in the shield so most of the stuff was already waiting. It had scanned Mima and Lolu and would have clothes and furs ready. No one would be able to tell the rich furs were synthetic.

The first supply floater came in with the dishes and Mima's tiara and necklace. The tiara had ten perfect emer-alds that were easily five carats apiece surrounded with smaller diamonds and rubies centering a twenty carat emerald.

The necklace matched each stone of the tiara perfectly and was hung on a chain of two carat perfect diamonds that entirely encircled Mima's neck.

There was a chest of perfect stones in fine settings for Lolu to select what she wanted along with a hundred kilos of gold bracelets, some plain and some set with stones. There were also hundreds of loose stones that could be sewed into any patterns she liked.

The next floater brought cloth in satin and lace spun with fine gold thread. The predominant colors were red and green and there was enough to cover all the furniture, make bedclothes and linens and have bolts enough left over to do the throne room.

Next was a load of artwork and statuary in precious metals inset with jewels where it was tasteful to do so. There were rich tapestries to hang around of slightly erotic scenes and hunting scenes.

Then came the food. Amaranth meal and rare delicate vegetables and seafoods taken from the deep waters near TR, gincha and spices.

"I'll have to send you the spoilables for each meal, but the amaranth, spices and gincha are dried and can be stored," TR reported. "I've planted gincha and amaranth on a large island so you can show where it came from if you ever have to. The natural physiologies for the plants are fine for this planet. I had to alter a few genes, but nothing important.

"I also planted some of that garlic stuff from Terra and some onions ditto. They're close enough and will give the food that extra zing, but remember they don't have breath deodorants here.

"There's some of that lacy parsley stuff that helps with most things, but not garlic. I doubt there's anything that works on garlic!

"Lopar's gathering a lot of lead so I'll be ready. You'll probably be asked to turn it all into gold, but I'm mining tons of the gunk. There's a mountain not far that's riddled with the stuff.

"My sensors tell me Lolu's coming up the stairs right now. I built a solar water heater and set it on the roof of your tower. It's a large iron tank with sand insulation. I won't use lead. You know the effects of that stuff after a few years so you can steer them away from using so much of it.

"They make some iron stuff so the tank's no big deal, but you'll have to figure how to use it on your shower."

The floaters sped out and rewelded the bars back over the windows seconds before Lolu came into the room. She saw all the stuff laying around and gasped. She hadn't ever seen anything one tenth so luxurious and had never known art could be that finely worked and colored. The metal-work was much finer than anything she'd ever seen and the tapestries were unbelievable in their detail.

Everything was in good taste – the jewels and baubles were in a closed chest of a dark reddish color with shining fittings and bands. The bed was covered with fine silk and satin and the cloth for dresses was in bolts of several colors. It was all far finer than anything that had ever been in that castle, though she'd heard of such things from travelers.

There were rich furs in silvery-gray, reddish brown, deeper brown and black. The jewels laid on the black fur laying on the green and gold bedcover made her gasp again. The fine foods on trays of pure silver and gold were fresh and smelled better than anything she'd known since she was a small child.

She stood speechless as she handed Tab the measure-ments for Mima. She stood staring around the room at it while Tab measured her. He stepped into the hallway for a few minutes and returned carrying fine dresses!

"This one is for Mima and these are for you," Tab instructed. "Those jewels are Mima's and these are yours. You can pick out whatever you want from that chest, as can Mima.

"I'd suggest you don't use too much at one time as that's cheap and gaudy-looking. We'll try to impress King Low Pants and Queen Hiccup that ostentation is *not* class.

"We're mostly going to have fun!"

Tab let Lolu look through all the fancy things, then sent her with Mima's clothes and jewels.

"I got all the gold and that crud you could ever want," the internals said. "You can let me know where and how much and all that crap. You'll have to arrange for me to be able to get it somewhere without being seen.

"I think this really *will* be a lot of fun! For all of us!"

Chapter one

Lolu came to him dressed in her finery when it was time to go to the dining hall for the evening meal. He smiled at her and noted that the famous good looks of the Kopett family hadn't missed her one bit!

He was programmed to notice such things and to even act on them.

A floater brought him a special wine, which he picked up and brought in with them.

They entered the hall and a dead silence fell – after the gasp from all the women who noticed the jewelry and fine furs Lolu was wearing. The material of Lolu's gown alone was worth a king's ransom and it had perfect stones sewn into the fabric across one shoulder and arm.

Mima had been instructed in the preparation of their food. There was a double seat to Lopar's right covered in the rich emerald-colored cloth with the ruby-red and gold pattern. Tab and Lolu strolled in a dead silence to the seat where he carefully removed her furs and hung them on a bracket that was placed for that purpose. He then sat and smiled at Lopar and Keenu, who was showing a barely controllable rage at Lolu, who was better and far finer dressed than she.

Then Mima entered pushing a cart with the dinnerware for Tab and Lolu. She was wearing a gown that was at least as fine as Lolu's and was sporting a stole of the rarest pure white terum from the ice packs to the north. The tiara and necklace were awesome as they sparkled and dazzled the assembly.

Mima placed the spun-gold placemats, taking care to see the light caught the jewels as she placed the plates and metalware. The blood-red cut crystal bowls were filled with a steaming soup made from a crustacean much like the lobster of Terra and a salad of bright fruits and leafy vegetables.

She then turned and regally pushed her cart out.

Tab poured the fine wine into the cut crystal goblets after tasting a few drops when he uncorked the bottle, which was also of the finest cut crystal.

He smiled into Lolu's eyes and raised his goblet. "To a warm and very exciting future!" he toasted and sipped the wine from Lolu's goblet while she took a sip from his.

There had been leaden silence throughout all this, but Keenu could take no more. "How ... how DARE you!" she screeched. "How dare you dress that kitchen slut in finery! How dare you bring that tramp into my presence dressed like some, some, some...! How DARE you!"

"Oh, I'm sorry!" Tab exclaimed. "I like nice things and want those who help me to have nice things.

"Lolu and I have developed an affection so I want her to have the best when we're in public places so I can be proud of her.

"Really now, it isn't very nice to call Mima a slut. She's a fine and honorable woman. She's not the one who spent all last evening in bed with Count Morest and this afternoon in bed with Bishop Loupe. You shouldn't call names that fit you better.

"As to `How dare I,' I dare anything I please! It's a pity you weren't raised with a little culture and manners. You could have as much – or more – but you simply aren't deserving.

"To put it in words you might understand, shut your damned mouth and eat!"

Lopar jumped to his feet and Tab expected another tirade from him, but he turned to Keenu.

"Loupe?!" he yelled in her face. "Even that prissy little fop? You would actually share bedchamber – you'd sleep with that effeminate little child molester?"

"Oh, they didn't sleep," Tab said, flippantly. "This soup is delicious, isn't it Lolu? I really must commend Mima. She's a genius with food!"

Another in fine robes who was seated next to Keenu waved at Lopar and stood.

"You seem to be rather much arrogant in your purported powers, alchemist," he said. "It was reported to me you can turn lead to gold." He clapped his hands and a team of guards entered pulling carts loaded with lead. "Here's some material for you to work with!"

Tab smiled at him and asked, "And exactly who the hells are you supposed to be?"

"I am called Feltron," he answered and bowed. "Let us watch your process of making lead into gold – if you can do such. I say you cannot and you will not! You are a charlatan and I will expose you as such. It is trickery and deceit.

"I challenge you to make good your foolish boasts!"

"Okay," Tab answered carelessly in turn. "Have the lead placed into the largest kettles you have and melted. We'll need lids for later for the kettles. Let me know when it's all liquid.

"You may then wish for me to explain how each of your own tricks are performed. A small child could learn any of them."

He placed the salad bowl and the soup bowl to the side as Mima entered with the cart, placed the empty bowls on the lower shelf along with the used flatware and placed a large platter with a pure silver cover in front of Tab. She handed him a carving knife and fork and stood with the cover lifted.

There was a golden loaf of the amaranth bread on the crystal platter, which he expertly sliced into, making a series of neat two-inch thick sections. Inside the loaf were baked several crisp vegetables and inside the vegetable layer was one of the large lobster-like tails. This was a favorite recipe from the Terran, Z. The aromatic spices filled the air as he cut the loaf. He then placed the platter back on the cart and handed the fork to Mima, who put two of the slices on each of Tab's and Lolu's plates. She then replaced the cover and opened another smaller server to take two perfectly baked clom roots in silver forceps, place one on each plate, slice it expertly open and put a dollop of cultured sour cream and the small flaked chives TR brought to plant on the island into the slice.

Mima then took the wine goblets and replaced them with cut clear crystal goblets of fine green tea, then rolled the cart out.

The lobster tail in amaranth loaf weighed over four kilos and the kitchen staff were dining on everything that wasn't served to Lolu and Tab. They'd just finished the salad and soup and all agreed they'd never eaten such fine food in their lives.

Tab thoroughly expected Keenu to explode in rage again, but she suddenly complained of a headache and left the room.

Tab called TR on internals and informed it the gold would be needed soon. He estimated there were six tons of lead in all the carts.

"They've got the lead out in the courtyard in big iron vats and're building fires around it," TR reported. "It'll take three and a half hours for it all to melt. I've got a small spy floater watching. The guards are complaining about all the work."

"They'll get the fires going good and break for a meal I would suppose," Tab replied. "They'll probably leave a guard or two to watch so you can put them to sleep or something and transfer the lead for the gold. I'll get a wire mesh screen to pour the lead through and it'll come out gold."

"Yo!" TR said.

Tab finished his meal and sat back while Lolu finished.

"Feltron," he said. "Is the lead getting hot yet?"

"It is being prepared," the sorcerer answered stiffly.

"Good," Tab said carelessly. "I'll get my light reactive piffledypoof glamyup cloosis and you can show me how it's being done. I'm sure even you can't screw up melting lead!

"Excuse me a moment, my dear. I must go to my rooms to get

the ingredients for my little recipe."

He stood and went to the tower where he picked up some talcum powder and salt and poured it carefully together into a jar in full view of the observer device that was put in while he was at dinner, then went back into the dining hall. Mima was standing uncertainly behind Lolu.

"Will yer be eatin' yer dessert, Sir?" she asked.

"In a moment, Mima," he answered. "You've done an excellent job with the meal. I have to process a little lead into gold for these lovely greedbags. It'll only take a few minutes, then I'll return for dessert and gincha brew.

"Excuse me one more time, my dear.

"Come, Feltron! Let's make some gold. I will wish to spend the rest of the evening without these distractions."

Feltron stared at him a moment, then led the way out to the courtyard where there were twelve large vats with fires raging around them.

"But they're not covered!" Tab exclaimed. "I *told* you we would need lids! They must be covered or the arghi barg will escape into the air and the feeblebush won't have a chance to verdigris! The entire crapola snapple goo will gangrenate into conglomerated defenestrated alpha smor-gasbord!"

"That is no problem!" Feltron cried. "Guards! The lids!

"We are not to be fooled so easily. I have prepared for any stalls you may wish to make."

The guards brought out the heavy lids for the vats and Tab poured a bit of the powder from the jar into each vat and told the guards to cover them quickly. The vats were not to be opened again until the moment to react them into gold. Exposure to air would prevent the reaction's taking place.

He and Feltron went back into the hall and Mima served their yellow sweetcake covered in crushed blueskin berries with sweet cream poured over it. She stood by until they finished their shortcake, then poured each of them a large green crystal cup of gincha brew.

"The guards took the lids off of two of the vats on orders brought from the hall. They left them off for about ten minutes then replaced them," TR reported on internals.

"Those two vats along with any others they may tamper with will have no gold, only lead," Tab instructed.

"Yo!" TR returned.

They finished the meal and watched as entertainers came in to play various instruments. Lolu knew the musicians. The crowd, who were feeling mellow now, asked her to sing. She took a lute-like instrument and sang and strum-med. She had a soft pleasant, mellow voice. Tab was enchanted.

They were then waiting and staring around at one another for half an hour or so when TR used the internals to say the vats were ready for him. Another had been accidentally uncovered for a couple of minutes, but that was lead, too.

"I believe the lead should be reacted by now," Tab announced offhandedly. "The Annenberg Quartet will have Dusseldorfed into the Aurora Borealis, which then melds and bids the canasta to the Aurora Australis in the Age of Aquarius, resulting in the gold glop.

"Shall we go out?"

They were led into the courtyard by Feltron, who had lost some of his bravado.

"Add a little dramatic suspense," TR suggested. "The third, fifth and sixth are lead. The fifth by accident."

Tab went to the closest vat, the sixth and knocked the plug out. He pulled a mesh from his robe, placed it in the hole and asked the guards to push a cart under the spout, then to tip the vat so it would pour.

Lead splashed into the cart.

"That vat was uncovered," Tab stated.

Feltron nodded sagely. This wasn't doing his nerves any good. He wanted to know if it worked and this alchemist had gone first to a vat he'd told the guards to uncover!

Tab went to the fifth vat and repeated the process. Lead.

"This vat's also been exposed!" Tab stated. "What's going on here? Your silly stupid trickery has cost me most of my supply of verdantly frimberlystump!"

"The first was exposed," Feltron announced. "This one was *not*! You are a fraud!"

"Crap!" Tab snapped. "This vat was exposed! Look! There's still soil on the lid! The lid was removed!"

A guard came to whisper into Feltron's ear.

"I have just been informed that a mountbeast came through and knocked the lid off of that vat," Feltron said. "This was not a part of our test."

"Just how many others have you used to reduce my supply of materials?" Tab snapped angrily.

"There is but one other. It is to you to find it," Feltron sneered. "Perhaps it will be the next one you choose?"

"It'll find itself!" Tab said caustically.

He moved along the row of vats, thumping each with a small stone he picked up. He stopped at number three and said, "This one. You have no conception of the fortune you've cost Lopar with this stupidity. He now has three vats of lead where he could have had three vats of gold. I'll let *him* handle the punishment for that idiocy!"

He went to vat number one where he repeated the mesh process. The guards tilted the vat down and gold filled the cart — and another! – and another!

"You'll have twenty one full cartloads of gold," Tab said to Lopar, who was drooling with greed along with Keenu, who had come to join the exhibition. "All the gold will now have to be poured through ... no! I'll turn the lead to gold in the vats, then you can melt it and pour it anytime you like."

He took a sword from a guard and wrapped the mesh around it, then knocked out the plug from each vat and swished the mesh around inside. He handed the guard his sword, which was thickly coated with gold.

"That's my gold!" Lopar cried.

"Don't be a greedy ass!" Tab demanded. "That much isn't enough to notice."

Lopar shut up, but it was plain he wasn't happy about it.

"This has been an exciting day, but I'm rather tired and now wish to retire," Tab announced. "I'll see you in the morning. Goodnight."

He took Lolu's arm and they strolled casually back into the castle. There was a hot bath waiting in the ground floor room!

"Mima said we were to arrange for a hot bath each evening here until you said to stop," Lolu said. "She made some of the soap you said you wanted this afternoon. It's here. It smells good!"

Tab had learned on one of his earliest assignments that he was designed to handle all aspects of interpersonal relationships and even had been noted as a superb lover by a Swaz female – and this girl was obviously expecting to stay here with him.

"I'm glad she had the presence of mind to make it a very large tub!" he said with a grin. "May I induce you to join me? We can wash those hard-to-reach areas for each other!"

She giggled and shed the gown. She was splashing in the tub before he even started to undress.

It was a great night!

In the morning Lolu asked whether she should wear the gold jewelry and fine gowns early in the day or would it only make Keenu mad.

"It's gross and low class to wear jewelry and gowns in the mornings," Tab tutored. "Not that I want to refrain in any way from angering Keenu. She won't get out of bed with whoever for a few hours yet so it doesn't matter.

"A very simple thing. No earrings, bracelets or brooches. A pastel scarf with a small pendant holding it on one shoulder and a very small cameo necklace in Cankth ivory and onyx on a thin gold chain. No more.

"Remember. Always quiet and simple in the morning. When we've taken a light midmeal, bracelets with a small brooch and very small pearl earrings. A quiet necklace like the opal beads or the turquoise. No emeralds, diamonds, rubies or other flashy stones before the evemeal. The smart woman would dress like you were dressed yesterday when I arrived in the morning. Add the earrings, a small bracelet and a scarf made of this beautiful green material with gold thread after the midmeal. It would go well with something white and brown for contrast. Fashion should be understated to be successful.

"You'll dress more simply this evening with understated jewelry and a simple gown that wraps your body tightly enough to show your exceptional figure and will use no makeup except for a slight coloring of the lips. I would suggest a pale pink or white to match the jewelry.

"We'll just have a small string of fire opals across the head above the eyes, small diamond earrings, the opal and ruby brooch to tie the wraps of the dress and the plain solid gold bracelet with a small emerald ring.

"Keenu will, of course, overdress in everything she's got and will appear the fool she is."

Lolu giggled and said, "You know I love to make a fool of that silly pfimewe, don't you?"

"I'd think any woman would enjoy that," Tab agreed. "Shall we go watch Lopar and Keenu drooling all over their gold?"

They went downstairs to the enormous kitchen where Mima was polishing the tableware.

"Don't go to a lot of trouble with that stuff, Mima," Tab said. "It only needs polishing every fifty days or so. It's got a permanent finish that retards tarnish and I can make more anytime we need it."

"Oh, NN Sir!" she replied. "I like to see it shine!"

"Ya din leave no orders 'bout bringin' breakfust so I din. I'll fix somethin' now."

"We'll have whatever's handy here," Tab said.

"Oh, NN Sir!" Mima cried. "It ain't fittin' you should eat inna kitchen! Ony th' servants eats inna kitchen, not the fine gennamen!"

"We aren't interested in that silliness," Tab replied. "We only act like that around Hiccup and Low Pants to show them for what they are.

"Riffraff!

"I like to eat with real folks. It's more like I remember from home when I was small. I like the small-talk and gossip and jokes we shared.

"I didn't hear anyone laugh last night. Not once. The only jokes were Hic and Low and that silly Feltbomb!"

Mima giggled and brought the sweetcakes and gincha.

"I'm gonna make some muffins with the flour ya done brought with the blueskin berries," Mima said. "I'll offer they'll be good! Yer kin put onna sweetcream if'n ya likes."

"Yes! That'll be great for the midmeal!" Tab suggested. "We'll have some of the seafood fried in butter in that sauce with all the spices and the tomato things.

"Just crush the tomatoes and heat them in a pan, add spices and squeeze the whole mess through the fine mesh, then simmer it until it's thick. Add some mountbeast radish and a few drops of vinegar and we'll dip the fried pieces of seafood in it. After that we'll have the muffins and green tea. We can eat in the kitchen spice garden so Queenie can look out her window and hate us!

"Very good idea, Mima!"

On his internals he asked TR why it had decided to introduce tomatoes.

"I didn't. They're a parallel evolution kinda thing," TR answered. "If you were organically a true Swaz instead of a lousy machine they'd kill you so fast you couldn't react. The digestive tracts of these people can easily process the poisons in them. They evolved with them.

"They look like tomatoes, they taste like tomatoes, but the plant isn't even close and the genetics are VERY different!"

After nibbling the sweetcakes and drinking the gincha Tab took Lolu into the courtyard where Lopar was super-vising the pouring of remelted gold into molds. He was running around scraping up the little drops that spilled and scraping the dregs from the molds before allowing them to be refilled.

"For crying aloud!" Tab snapped. "You have on the order of five tons of the stuff! What's the object of scraping a half gram here and there?"

"It's all mine!" Lopar cried. "Gold, and it's all mine! I will finally have enough to ... do some things! I need it all! There is so much more than anyone knows. I must have it all and more! I must! I have so much to do! This is the start, not the ending! You will see! You will see Lopar is *not* the petty person people think he is! You will see!"

Tab and Lolu laughed and strolled toward the gate where Lolu said she wanted to help Mima for a little while so Keenu wouldn't start causing her grief. Tab said he'd handle any giving of grief if Keenu or anyone else bot-hered his friends, kissed her lightly and went on to Wooler's pub.

"I hear you turned the whole stinking castle into pure gold," Wooler greeted.

"I made a few tons of it," Tab agreed with a grin.

"Could you make me some?" Wooler asked.

"Sure!" Tab replied. "Get all the lead you can find and melt it down in a covered vat and I'll turn it to gold for you. It's really very easy to do, you know.

"I think you should study things a bit before you ask for more than is good for you, but I'll make whatever you want."

"Are you serious?" Wooler asked.

"Yes, surely," Tab answered. "It's a nice metal to have at times. It has its uses."

Wooler shook his head and went out. A few minutes later he came back in and said he'd signaled for the guards to come. Tab grinned and ordered beer and melon. The guard came in after a few minutes and Wooler had a long conversation with them. They left and Wooler came over.

"I know what you're doin' now," he said. "I'm gonna help – 'sides! I always wanted a bunch'a gold!"

They talked awhile. Tab said he'd come tonight and for them to have all the lead they could find melted and ready in covered vats.

"What the hell are you doing to me?!" TR snapped through the internals. "I've got to gather all that gold and dump all that lead!"

"You know perfectly well what I'm doing here don't you?" Tab sent back. "Besides! All you do is squat on the bottom and send servos to do the actual work!"

"Yo!" TR replied. "It might even work. I sort of like this kind of thing, don't you?

"Of course I don't get to sleep with the hot broads, but we can't have everything.

"You sort of like that, don't you?"

"I sort of enjoy the hell out of that!" Tab sent back. "I'll say Maita did a great job on me there! I can fit right into this kind of society."

"You're disgusting!" TR said.

"Why?" Tab asked. "It's the norm for this culture."

"I was just thinking how Z would react, but even he's begun to change there. He's not so inhibited anymore," TR answered. "I'll get the crap ready for you."

Tab went back to the castle room where he designed and made a trough for his shower, hung it, made a water lift, laid out the whole delivery system and finished it up. He could step out on his balcony over the river (He had to remove the barred door), pull a bucket rope and the water would fall through a screen. All he had to do was get the water twenty eight meters up to the roof from the river.

Easy! He got plenty of heavy rope, made a pulley tripod and hung it above the tank. He then made a loop across the pulley with a big bucket on each end. As he raised one bucket he lowered another one. The buckets held about six gallons, so five trips up on the pulley filled the tank. His strength made it easy, but it would take two men after he was gone if he could get these people into the habit of bathing regularly.

Mima brought the midmeal into the cool spice garden. It was probably delicious, but being a machine he wasn't a good judge. He and Lolu sat on a wide flat rock and laughed and toasted one another while Keenu stood behind her curtains and glared.

After lunch Tab went to finish up his project and to make new plans with TR. Now that they'd decided how to handle this thing it would have to move slowly and smoothly and would have to be good enough to become self-perpetuating. He was beginning to have mixed feelings about Lopar since the meeting in the courtyard that morning. It was perhaps because he felt Lopar wanted all the gold to be able to get away from Keenu. Anyone who wanted to escape such as her couldn't be all bad!

Every time he came across Keenu, his low opinion of her was strengthened more. She was totally worthless to the race and to anything else. She was selfish, greedy, lacking in compassion, arrogant, spoiled and everything else negative he could think of. If what he heard was half true she was also sadistically cruel. She reminded him of an Immin, but the last thing he ever wanted to think of again was Immins! He sincerely hoped the last of those had killed each other off in their exile and the sore on the galaxy that was the Immin race would heal.

Lolu came up and they dressed for dinner.

They entered the dining hall and went to their seats. Lolu was dressed in a wraparound sheath of gold and maroon with very small enameled earrings, a small silver and turquoise ring and a very tasteful small ruby brooch with a small dark green scarf hanging across her shoulder to clasp the dress wraps in place. She had a touch of yellow/ bronze lip color and a small opal bead on a very thin gold chain across her forehead just below the crest. She was elegant and poised as she smiled at Keenu and took her seat. Keenu had her two emeralds on display with huge plates of gold obviously cast that day weighing her head down. Every piece of jewelry she owned was somewhere on her along with enough gold to make it difficult for her to even move. She stared in disbelief as Lolu smiled and talked with Tab. She whispered to Lopar and left.

"It seems Keenu has another headache," Tab noted.

"I don't wonder!" Lolu replied. "She has to be carrying at least twenty kilos of gold around! I feel sorry for her."

"Don't," Tab protested. "She's not worth it.

"Ahhh! Here's our dinner!"

Mima was dressed in dark green with gold thread pat-terns and a black fur hat. She had a small dangling diamond earring on one ear and a string of pale white opals on a necklace. She was as elegant as Lolu.

Mima placed the bowls of salad and soup in front of them and waited as Tab poured white wine he brought, then went back to her cart.

The soup was a clear broth with flakes of herbs floating on it. Tab could tell it was delicious from Lolu's reaction so would remember to compliment Mima.

When they sat their bowls aside Mima brought out the main course. It was a fowl much like pheasant that had been cooked with sweet butter, onions, a spice like thyme and another like oregano and floated in a bath of tart white wine in a closed pan. The bird was taken from the soak pan when done and quickly browned in a hot oven. It was served with several vegetables, one of which was in a sweet cheese sauce.

Dessert was a thin sheet of amaranth dough rolled in morktht butter, sugar, bits of fruits and nuts and sprinkled with rare spices, then baked until it was a golden brown. It was perfect with gincha brew.

As they were basically ignored throughout the meal they made no excuses when they got up and walked out to stroll casually toward Wooler's pub, then to the guard offices.

There were two vats of melted lead. Tab threw some powder into the vats and quickly replaced the lids.

"Let's all go back to Wooler's and have a cool beer or two," Tab suggested. "We have to wait a couple of hours and nothing's going to happen until then."

They went back to wait until TR said the gold was in the vats, then Tab said, "Let's go catalyze our gold. I'm tired and want to get to bed."

Lolu giggled.

They went to the vats where Tab swished the mesh around in the gold, then they poured it into a row of molds so they could divide it evenly.

"We decided to make enough so's everbody who don't live at the castle can get their own block uh it," Wooler explained. "If everbody's got some you done what you wanted, right?"

"You got that right!" Tab agreed. "Come on, Lolu. We have a hot bath waiting."

As they strolled toward the castle Lolu asked him what Wooler meant about getting what he wanted.

"The only reason that gold's worth anything is because there isn't much of it," Tab explained. "Now there are many tons of it here so it isn't worth much anymore. Lopar has about two thirds of what's here so he has two thirds of very little. You can picture how he'll react when he sees that."

They took their bath and went to bed.

Feltron was waiting for them in the dining hall when they came to breakfast. He was insulted when they insisted on eating in the kitchen until Tab gave him a cup of gincha. He couldn't believe how good it tasted.

"What did you want to see me about?" Tab asked.

"I want to know how you transmute lead into gold!" Feltron replied sharply.

"Why?" Tab asked innocently.

"Why?!" Feltron cried, staring in shocked disbelief at Tab. "I could use a little wealth! It would advance me well ahead in my studies!"

"Do you know I made tons of gold for the townspeople?" Tab asked.

"Yes! So what?" Feltron shot back.

"It's not worth much when everyone has all they want," Lolu said. "I thought you were supposed to be smart. I could figure that out!"

Feltron's mouth dropped open.

"Why don't you get your, er, friends to show you how to make gold and jewels?" Tab asked.

"What friends?" Feltron asked.

"You didn't make that wand and you didn't make the watcher devices," Tab replied. "You didn't make carbon steel. If your friends are all that good as alchemists they should be able to show you those simple things.

"I'm very surprised an alchemist would aid a sorcerer."

"I never had any help!" Feltron said stubbornly. "I made the wand myself."

"Okay," Tab replied. "You show me how to make a wand like that and I'll show you how to make the gold and jewels."

"No! No! I'm not showing anyone how to make a wand!" Feltron snapped.

"I didn't think you would," Tab said. "Come, Lolu. Let's go for a walk. I'd like to see what Wooler and friends are doing with all that gold."

They left with Feltron trying to figure some way to get the secret method of transmutation from Sir Northram. Tab used the internals to tell TR to watch Feltron very closely. "He'll very damned well try to get in touch with whoever gave him that wand now!"

Wooler served them green tea in gold cups. "I talked all'a the guys into makin' everday dishes outta tha gold," Wooler said. "I 'spect Lopar's gonna seize alla it anyhow so that'll reduce him ta grabbin' people's dishes.

"You said it were gonna be fun – 'n it is! So far."

"Just be sure everyone knows it's not worth fighting for," Tab advised. "If it's too easy Lopar will feel that much more the fool."

"Hee! Why not make gold seats for the outhouses?" Lolu asked. "That would really be something to see! Lopar taking outhouse seats!"

"Yuh-huh, but would ya wanna sit on no gold seat inna colder weather?" Wooler asked. "NN done said we gotta think about alla those things 'fore we do 'em."

A pair of guards came in and sat to talk. They said they'd

thought about making solid gold shields, but they were 'way too heavy and a blade or lance would go right through them so they made dishes like Wooler suggested.

One said his mate made picture frames from all of theirs. She made needlework pictures to hang around the house and to give to friends so it would make for nice gifts. Feltron had offered them vast riches if they'd find Sir Northram's process for them, but they said they had more riches than they knew what to do with now. Feltron had stormed off in fury, swearing and making curses at them.

"Uh crossed muh fingers like thet thar 'n said 'far minzaper strukenfloog' er somethin' like thet thar uh made up 'n 'e sez whut wuz I doin' 'n I done sez Sir Northram done give us 't spell whut turns back uh curse ta tha giver!" one of the guards said. "Ya should'a seed 'im run! 'E wuz still swearin' – but 'e weren't givin' no more curses!"

"He knowed he was beat!" Wooler agreed. "He don't know nothin' about what NN can do an' he knows he ain't got no way to fight the science thing with no magic, least not with no magic he knows nothin' about!"

They talked and joked for awhile, then went along to the shoe shop where Tab bought Lolu a pair that would be ready for her the following morning.

They then went back to the castle where Tab finished work on his shower and filled the tank. He would know by evening if the solar collector would work. He was sure it would and that the insulated tank would keep him in warm water a full day if it was cloudy.

He was working on a way to pipe running water into the rooms when TR said Feltron was planning to go for a ride.

"How?" Tab asked.

"Got a double team of mountbeasts to pull him in a carriage. He's taking food for a week so we're about to find out where the aliens are here. We'll also find out what they are and what they want – maybe.

"I can plant bugs when we find them.

"My floaters haven't found anything, but I don't know where to look. They aren't using any broadcast energy to trace and I can't find a ship with the floaters unless it's using a hell of a lot of power for something. These will know better than that because this kind of planet is auto-matically restricted."

"Keep on it, TR," Tab replied. "It's probably some new race in space who don't know about culture damage."

He finished building the shower and had everything right so he explored the castle and was surprised to find it had a fair library. He spent two hours absorbing all the books there.

Another room was filled with art, some of it good. He'd seen evidence of artistry before so that was expected, though he was surprised Keenu and Lopar had such good taste.

He strolled into a courtyard garden and Keenu came out toward him. "We seem to have gotten off to a bad start together," she gushed coyly. "I know I must appear to be some kind of fool to you, but I've been cooped up in this place for six years and am going mad! It's too much for an active woman such as I."

She took his arm and leaned against him.

"It must be frustrating," Tab agreed coldly.

"Oh! You don't know!" she whined. "Lopar does try to be a good husband, but I wasn't born to live isolated like this! I was born to travel and meet people. I was born to see the whole world, not just this little piece of it! I was born to much greater things! I *must* get away from here!"

She was pressing against him and rubbing his back with one hand.

"Rule has its rules," Tab said. "You have responsibilities and must remain strong to meet them."

She dropped the pretense and pushed him down on a bench. "I

need a strong man!" she wailed. "I have my needs, too! I'm not some statue just because I'm queen!

"Take me! Make me a whole woman!"

"There aren't any twenty men who can fill your needs," Tab answered conversationally. "I really couldn't sleep with a woman who would lay with that child-molesting fop, Loupe."

He stood and nodded to her, then turned his back and walked off. She was still screaming obscenities as he went back into the castle to prepare for midmeal. He saw movement to one side of the hall and went over.

Lopar was inside. He had been watching the garden.

"I don't want her," Tab remarked as he walked by.

"I don't either," Lopar replied. "I married her and I'm stuck. A king can't divorce. She'll sleep with anyone who can spare the time and energy. I'm as bad as she is so I guess we deserve each other. I'm as drawn to wealth as she is to sex.

"I've made quite the fool of myself and you've taught me a valuable lesson. I went into the town to buy a number of things in the trade shops, but they wouldn't accept gold in payment. They say they have too much already and can't think of what to do with it except to make dishes.

"A great problem has arisen now. Gold has very little value anymore. What am I to use for commerce?"

"I wish I thought you really have learned the lesson," Tab said. "You could become a worthwhile king and could be remembered in history for thousands of years."

"How's that?" Lopar asked. "I'll admit there's no reason you should believe anything I say. This is the first time I remember ever having to think for myself. I've spent my whole life trapped in the role of a king and realize it's something I'm really not psychologically prepared to be."

"I'll take a chance on you," Tab replied. "Gold isn't worth any-thing – here – but it's still the basis of money everywhere else.

You have a couple of ships and have good roads.

"Take the gold, buy worthwhile things from the whole world and concentrate them here. Great art. Books. Knowledge of any kind. These are the things with real value. Make this kingdom the safe repository of the world's knowledge and you'll draw the greatest alchemists and the newer scientists. You can return your first investments many times over and can ensure the future of this kingdom.

"Let there be something positive to find here. Value is tied to rarity, as you've seen. Gold isn't rare and the market for it changes all the time.

"Knowledge, on the other hand, is always in great demand and short supply and always will be. Its value always is rising so preserve and concentrate it here. Make strong fortress libraries to keep the knowledge safe for all time to ensure the future of the world.

"You'll need a copy of every book made. It doesn't matter how poor the book is, a single copy should be preserved. You can also have librarians who catalog everything. If alchemists and scientists are here when they make their discoveries you can get a part of the profits from the discoveries.

"I've made an interior shower.

"You can start a thing called a patent. I'll tell you how it works and your court will be the final word on all patents in the world.

"Oh, yes! This could be the best thing that could happen to you."

Lopar nodded. "It could be," he said. "I will think on it. As you say, these things have value that will never go away while you have shown how false a thing security in gold is.

"I have heard of these patents."

Lopar walked off with his hands clasped behind his back, lost in thought.

"I begin to wonder if he *is* capable of being more than he is?"

Tab asked TR on the internals. "What was that part about patents? What have you found?"

"It's the right part of history for them here," TR replied. "I think there's something about patents in one of those books in the library."

Tab went into the dining hall but no one was there so he went to his tower to "invent" a form of electric light. He'd read in the library that some research had been done with electric sparks making certain rare gases glow. These people were going to start off with the florescent light. They already knew about organic phosphors and coated screens that would glow and about natural fluorescence. They knew that electricity would arc very easily through mercury vapor.

He could use a standard coil starter, a drop of mercury, rare gases and a phosphor-coated tube. It was all stuff they already had. He would merely be the first to combine the things. That was the basis of invention and well might stimulate the natural inventors among the people.

They had hand-driven piston pumps and they had a crude steam engine. He could combine the two things to make a piston pump to lift water to his tank on the roof.

He'd have to stop short of the electric motor because they didn't have anything strong enough to logically work from.

"Feltron's going into the west mountains," TR reported.

"Send some spy floaters to find what's in there," Tab instructed. "Be discreet. They might have sensors to detect floaters."

He worked a glass tube in a gas flame to form the neon tube bulb. He would coat the inside of the tube with phosphors. The tube, gas burner and phosphors were all things TR was sending over by floater, things that were gathered from a city a quarter of the way around the world. They were actually native products so there was no risk whatever in using them. There was also a small tank of neon.

All those products were from an industrial city Tab read about in the books. The various gases were produced by a large piston compressor there and stored in the tanks. Iron was refined and formed there, as was copper and glass. The steam engine Tab would copy was like one they used to run the compressor. There was a lot of neon and argon in the atmosphere of the planet so they could get quite a bit. Oxygen and carbon dioxide liquefied out of the compressed air with relative ease and the natives had worked out several methods to separate the rare gases from the nitrogen because nitrogen definitely did NOT liquify easily!

TR had put tags on all the supplies in the language of the industrial city. Tab would say he bought all the stuff from a trade schooner.

"Maybe I should invent the steamboat," Tab suggested.

"Don't invent the steamboat," TR sent. "How could you tie it in to anything? You could use the steam engine to run your pump, but you.... Hey! I can do better than a steam-boat! I'll make a jet boat! Pump the water out through a nozzle! They use nozzles on their fire brigade pumps to increase the pressure! It's another two things they already have except your pump will be run by the steam engine and the water will be run through a restricting nozzle.

"It's crud they have, you'll just do it first. Like you did on Hellrun."

"Are you certain they have anything that sophisticated?" Tab asked.

"I'm sorting all that stuff from those books you read," TR replied. "I found diagrams by a guy named Gardan at Work City. I'll input the whole thing. Here."

Tab received a quick fastpulse burst containing the information from the castle library Tab had sent to TR. TR had sorted and indexed everything and sent it back to Tab for use.

Tab sat at his desk to draw the plans for the pump, working

directly from Gardan's diagrams, adding that to the boat drawing he made. He was surprised when the floater came to cut its way in at the window.

"Put the damned bars back up, Stupid!" Tab demanded. "Or did you forget we permanently removed the bars to the balcony door?"

"No, I didn't forget anything, Smartass!" TR replied. "I thought it'd be a tiny tad smarter to come in the window on the far side instead of through the balcony, which is being watched. I'll be happy to put the bars back and come around!"

Tab grinned and took the things for the light off the tug floater, which went back out and replaced the bars.

"I've got to make a generator first anyhow," he mumbled as he put the things on a shelf. "The ones they have will run the light but they're not very efficient. They run off of steam engines."

He turned back to his sketches.

Lolu came to him to tell him it was time to go to the dining hall. He had her dress moderately and they went to their seats. Lopar leaned toward him and said, "I would speak with you about building a book repository. I see the way to build another place where alchemists can come at my expense to work on things that seem most likely to produce positive results."

"Yes! A wonderful idea!" Tab replied. "A place to centralize study and research will advance the kingdom rapidly to the forefront of civilization. It might be as well to build a large theater that'll attract the best talent. The theater will attract talent, the talent attracts the wealthy, the wealthy attract ever better talent and funds are thus generated for the kingdom. It wouldn't be too long before this kingdom could be known as the cultural center of the world – *and* the research center!"

Lopar nodded and sat back in thought.

Keenu made her entrance and had actually made herself up in good taste. She sneered at Tab and sat ignoring him the rest of the evening.

"I've taught her the proper way to dress for the occasion," Lolu said, leaning close to him. "I doubt anyone could teach her to conduct herself as more than a common whore, though."

Tab agreed and they had a very pleasant meal and a pleasanter evening walking along the river discussing the stars, the world and other inconsequentialities.

In the morning Tab began the construction of his pump. He was able to obtain a fire pump and make a small steam engine that was leaky and inefficient, but that worked in a barely acceptable manner. It was the following afternoon when he called all who wanted to watch and started the pump. It filled the shower tank and he let it keep running long enough to have a sheet of water pouring off the roof.

He shut it off.

"What is the practical value of this?" Lopar asked.

"We'll build a tank on the roof and use the pump to fill it when it's low," Tab answered. "We can make copper or brass pipes to carry water to the kitchen, to my shower and to your quarters and another pipe to carry the used water to the river downstream from the castle. That way the used water won't ever recirculate through the system. We can have a rubber cap on the ends of the pipe in each place that can be pinned shut to stop the water and opened when you need water at that place."

"NN, Sir!" Mima called. "Whyn't put beer keg valves in tha pipes so's ya kin jest pull ta handle fer water?"

"That's a wonderful idea, Mima!" Tab called back. "It's so easy – and we don't have to design anything new.

"You see, Lopar? All you have to do is pull the handle and you have water right in your personal quarters! We can put a white tank in the shade and a black one in the sun and can have warm water for the bath by simply pulling the handle. Think of all the uses, particularly in the cold times! You have water in your own quarters by pulling a beer keg handle! No other castle in the world will have that kind of luxury!"

"Indoor pipes?" Lopar asked. "Water inside when you want it? Even warm? This alone will advance us far over the other countries. This will be the place to live for the better educated and wealthy. To think of the luxury – and everyone can have it. Everyone! All citizens in the town will have a luxury no one else in the highest classes will have anywhere else on the face of the world!

"Could we also make a very large tank up on the hill and make pipes so everyone can have water from one place? We will only have to pump water to the one tank and the fact that water will always seek the lowest level will make it run down into the town.

"You see? I saw you in my library. I *do* read all my books. I read every new book I can get. I always have loved reading and learning new things. We could make a very large copper vat with a gas fire under it and have both warm and cool water. The *luxury* of that! I can picture so many uses!"

"I'm afraid the water would cool in the pipes before it got to town," Tab cautioned. "It's a wonderful idea though."

"No, no!" Lopar cried. "We bury the pipes! All iron pipes can be wrapped in the center of a meter of concrete that will keep the warmth for a long while! It can be done! I know it can be done! They make the iron pipes and copper tanks in Work City and we have the gold to buy all we want.

"You see why I wanted more gold? It wasn't so much my greed, though I was greedy and make no denials about that, as I want to improve things.

"It *can* be done! I *know* it!"

"It might work," Tab agreed. "Think about it! The citizens of this kingdom can bathe every day if they want! We'll be the envy of all others in the world!"

"Get the hell out of there and be ready for one of the worst miserable damned shocks in your existence!" TR sent over the internals. "Feltron is almost where he's going and I've already seen enough to be as mad as Maita is – and, great spinning galaxies, is Maita mad! Furious!

"I contacted Maita first thing. Get away for a few days! Now! Any damned excuse or no damned excuse!"

Tab looked at Lopar, who was staring at him, and said, "I was lost in thought. I have to make some plans if you're to build the public water supply and the research center and the theaters you'll also have to build housing for all the people who'll come.

"I have an idea for using the pumps to move a ship! With steam power!

"The new large inns will have the pipes already built-in when the buildings are constructed. The wealthy will vacation here to experience the luxury of water in the rooms. All suites will have flowing water, warm and cool.

"I can see it! The educated will flock to this place!

"We have one problem though."

"What is it?" Lopar asked.

"We'll need much more gold to pay for it. The inns will need furniture and rugs and that sort of thing and shops will.... I'm going to leave for a few days to gather the beta-frobishing flooble and the flottiewatt to transmutate more gold from lead. I'll leave immediately! Have more lead ready when I return, but you can measure and order the pipe and iron we'll need. You've shown you have the ability to figure it out. The cool tank can be staved like a large barrel.

"We'll need about five more tons of lead. We don't want to make so much more gold that it'll ruin its value elsewhere so people here will have to agree not to speak of the amounts we have. It would harm them as well as the kingdom.

"I'll go immediately! Have the lead ready when I return!"

Page 55

He turned and trotted off before anything else could be said. He knew of only one thing that could throw Maita into a fury. It left a cold knot inside of him.

"I really think Lopar is neither stupid nor nearly as bad as I thought," he sent to TR as he trotted toward his room.

Chapter two

Tab went directly to his tower, grabbed the "shield" floater and headed out. Lolu ran to him and he told her he was expecting her to keep the tower in order until he returned. She couldn't understand why he had to leave in such a hurry.

"I may be too late already," he said. "The flottiewatt only blooms once every seven years and it's very near the end of the season. If I don't get it now we do without for that long. I have to do this while Lopar's in the mood or it may be lost forever.

"I'll only be a few days, I hope."

He didn't feel in the least bit guilty about the lie and kept moving. He was soon back downstairs and headed for River Road. He heard Lopar ask Lolu what the emergency could be.

"Northram must collect a certain plant," she explained. "It won't bloom again for seven years and without it he can't make the gold trans ... powder stuff that makes it work.

"He must hurry because the season is almost over. He says we must have the gold now, not seven years too late!"

Tab went to River Road where he saw one of the guards who had been at the "transmutation" and Wooler running toward him so he stepped into the forest and climbed across the floater. It took him away at terrific speed among the large boles of the trees.

He soon reached the river where the floater headed directly upstream. TR was controlling the floater as it knew every inch of the trail Tab would have to follow.

"Okay, TR," Tab sent. "What's the big scare? – like I don't know!"

"You're gonna see soon enough. Maita's so mad I won't be one bit surprised to see it here!" TR replied.

The floater was moving more than two hundred kilo-meters per

Page 57

hour and soon turned from the river through a canyon into the mountains that were growing ever higher.

"I'm trying to get you in there before Feltron reaches the place," TR said. "He's pretty close, but those mountbeasts are slow. He'll have to dismount from his carriage soon and climb about a kilometer through rough scrub.

"It's about sixty kilometers more. You'll be there first, but just barely.

"Hang on tight!"

Tab waited until the floater slowed and went closer to the ground. He was laid across the floater in a position no organic being could have tolerated, but sat up now that the wind drag wouldn't make any difference.

"I'm going to keep you low and bring you up behind and above the place," TR explained. "There's a sharp cliff just behind them they won't have sensors on.

"You go ahead by foot for a few meters now. You can ride the floater down when you decide it's best."

He followed TR's instructions and came to a small floater on the edge of the cliff. It was observing and recording what was happening below.

There was a standard research dome attached to the entrance of a standard empire small explorer spacecraft sitting under a dense camouflage cover.

"I guess Maita IS hot!" Tab said. "That's an empire ship!"

"That's not half why Maita's furious and you damned well know it!" TR snapped.

Tab studied the way before him. It was a sheer cliff.

He climbed off his floater and went around to the side where the footpath Feltron must take came in. He irised the floater in and held it like a shield. He waited until he saw the sorcerer coming. When he was close he went to meet him.

"Hello Feltron," Tab greeted. "I see you had to run to your

friends for advice!"

"How did you get here!?" Feltron cried.

"I walked," Tab answered. "It's much closer if one follows a straight line instead of the road."

Feltron stared at him.

"Okay. I flapped my arms and flew like a bird," Tab said.

Feltron still stared.

"If I told you you wouldn't believe me," Tab said. "Go on back to King Lopar. You have no business dealing with the evil forces here. It's no one's business if you sell your own spirit, but you endanger everyone in the kingdom and you know it. Go back or I'll kill you!"

"No!" Feltron yelled. "I made contract with the star-people and they will protect me! They have promised! Get out of my way!"

"You fool!" Tab yelled. "They didn't even show you how to make gold! They're using you and they couldn't care at all if I kill you!

"Go back to Lopar!"

The noise of the argument would be heard at the space-ship and they could expect company soon. Tab wasn't at all sure he could fool those aliens. They might recognize the floater for what it was, but he couldn't suddenly disap-pear now. That would be much too suspicious.

Feltron started to move toward the spaceship again and Tab turned to see they were observed – by an Immin!

Tab managed not to show any reaction. He'd expected it as soon as TR said Maita was furious.

He could understand why Maita would be livid. Maita and the crew thought they were free of Immins. All of them were supposed to be on Orta under quarantine.

Tab placed his hands into a mystic sign from the planet and cried, "Begone, evil one! Back to the dark regions! Take your evil from this place!"

The Immin stared at him and spoke to Feltron. "What is the meaning of bringing this creature here? We told you you must not betray us to others!"

"No! I didn't know he was following me!" Feltron cried. "I didn't see him until right now!"

The Immin shot Tab with a stun beam so he pretended to be knocked unconscious.

"Leave him there," the Immin ordered. "He won't be conscious for a couple of hours. I'll send Cape to finish him off.

"What are you doing here?"

"Why won't you show me how to make gold?" Feltron asked. "He made so much it isn't worth anything in the kingdom anymore!"

"That's impossible!" the Immin snapped. "You can't make gold or anything else! It's a trick!"

"It is not! I saw it!" Feltron cried. "He made five tons of it at once in front of thirty four people and all the guards! He made it for the shopkeepers and the housekeepers! Everybody has so much they don't know what to do with it!

"Here! Is this gold?" He handed the Immin a large bar of pure gold.

"It seems to be, but gold isn't worth anything to us so we don't really much care. We can't have the economy ruined here though. Not yet," the Immin said.

Feltron asked, "What do you mean 'not yet?' You said you would show me how to become king and to be rich! What do you mean?"

"We use a different economic standard, not gold," the Immin answered. "Come to the dome. They'll explain how it works."

As soon as they were out of sight Tab stood and went into the forest where he made his way close to the dome. Feltron was sitting on a bench in front of the dome and the Immin who came to shoot him with the stunner came out of the door with a male.

She pointed to the footpath and turned to Feltron and said something. Even with his enhanced hearing he couldn't hear so he moved around to where he could move close behind them. Feltron was just saying something about his making the gold.

"...some powder in and said you couldn't allow the air to hit it. The guards put the lids on and we went inside. I had guards watching every second and from four different places. I had the guards take the lids off of two vats for a few minutes and put them back on.

"When we poured it there was gold except in the two vats that had been opened and one more, but the guards told me a mountbeast had knocked the lid off of that vat and they put it right back on."

"You mean the third vat, the one accidentally opened, was lead?" the Immin asked. "You say even you didn't know it had been opened?"

"Yes, yes!" Feltron said. "That's exactly what I said! No one knew it was opened except the four guards watching and the rider on the mountbeast who helped put the lid back on! The guards and rider wouldn't say anything because they would be disciplined for allowing the mount-beast to be so close to the vats and the rider would be disciplined for being so damned clumsy. Lopar would have them beat for it!

"You have to teach me how to make gold, Xut! You have to!"

"I would have said it couldn't be done," Xut replied. "It had to be trickery of some sort.

"What's the matter with Cape?"

The Immin male who had been sent to finish Tab off came at a run across the little meadow from the path shouting, "He's gone! There's no one anywhere along the path!"

"This is some kind of trickery!" Xut yelled. "Kik! Come out here! Now!"

Another Immin female came from the dome and asked, "What

the hell's the commotion?"

"Something's not right here!" Xut said. "That sorcerer made gold out of lead in front of fifty people, tons of it. Now he disappears after being shot with a fully charged stunner! We have to find out what's happening! This is getting out of hand before we even know about it! Find that damned sorcerer! Get everyone on it! Send out the search floaters! Get that sorcerer! I want him alive! Move!"

"He's not a sorcerer!" Feltron shouted. "Didn't you even hear me? He's *not* a sorcerer, he's an alchemist!"

"What the hell's the damned difference?" Cape asked.

"Alchemists don't use magic," Feltron shot back. "They use something called science. I use magic! You can't transmute with magic! It has to be done with science!"

The Immins had a short discussion, then Xut released several spy floaters that went out along the entrance path. There were four Immins watching individual holovision screens directing the floaters.

"TR! Find the wavelengths of those floaters and give them a show on their video receptors!" Tab sent through the internals. "Make it something that'll scare the piss out of that bitch!"

The master video screen was brought out showing what all the floaters were "seeing" on a large split screen. The Immins and Feltron were watching. Tab focused on it with his zoom vision to see what TR would do.

Nothing happened for a few minutes longer, then there was some sort of motion on a screen in the corner. Xut expanded the master screen to hold that screen and directed the floater toward the motion – and there he was!

Xut sent the other floaters to the area as Tab looked up to see the first one watching him. He took a small object from his pocket and pointed it at the camera. The screen went blank.

"How the nine hells!?!?" Cape yelled. "Didn't you shield the damned floater?"

"Certainly! Shut up!" Xut demanded. "We have to learn how he does it. He claims it isn't magic."

"The others are still working," Kik pointed out.

Two more floaters had him at two different angles. He was walking along a path that led out onto a promontory over the road. He glanced up to see the floater to his left, drew some signs in the air with his finger, the signs hung in the air as bright flames – seen by two floaters. Tab blew lightly against the flames and they moved toward the floater. *That* screen went dead.

"Damn!" Cape screeched. "That's impossible! Those floaters are fully shielded – and that ain't no science! It's magic, pure and simple!"

"Are you really killing those spy floaters?" Tab asked on the internals.

"Yo!" TR replied. "I got floaters of my own out there and the E-shields on those survey floaters are worthless against them."

The last floater was watching Tab from behind some shrubbery. He sat on a rock to watch the road for a few minutes, stood, spread his arms, spun, glowed brightly and disappeared!

Tab got an idea then. They were all staring at the screen in sheer disbelief so he came silently to stand looking over Kik's shoulder at the big screen.

"Did I miss one of your devil machines?" he inquired. "I see that is where I left a moment ago."

Kik squealed and Xut screamed. Cape spun and drew a sonic stunner.

"I wouldn't!" Tab snapped and pointed at the stunner. Cape froze.

"Put the devil thing away!" Tab ordered. "It can't harm me."

"You're to go from this world! Leave Klemmr! I sense you are evil and I warn you you have no power over me! Get in your machine and go back to the dark region between the stars or I'll call the light of the inner sun to consume you!

"Defy me at your peril!"

"How would you, as you say, 'call the light of the sun' to this cold world?" Kik sneered. "There are some things that are way beyond your magic and that is definitely one of them."

"The light and heat of the sun is caused from the joining of two alike things to make a different thing," Tab replied. "I'll make the alike things in your devil machine come together to make lead. It is a simple thing. It will produce heat and the devil machine will be consumed as will all things near.

"I warn you!"

"That fool can cause a fusion reaction with TK!" Cape cried in Maitan. "That's how he made the gold! He's the most powerful TK talent we've ever found! He could make crihcht dust out of the Acnians! Damn it to hell! What do we do?"

"Do not speak in alien tongues!" Tab demanded sharply. "Your evil spells will not work here! I can turn them back against the sender! Beware!"

Kik suddenly drew her laser and fired at him, but he saw it coming and ducked. Feltron jumped up and she shot him full in the face.

"That was a mistake!" Tab said in Maitan. "I don't have to put on an act anymore.

"How the hells did you damned Immins get off of Orta?"

"Who are you?" Xut screeched.

"I'm Tabori R. DeSixtee, adviser and special investigator to Emperor Maita. You'll possibly recall I was among those who were responsible for Immins being defeated and quarantined on Orta. I think Tabori R. DeSixtee and the Acnian, Rollo, are two names every Immin alive would know!

"No Immin will live to leave this planet. This is exactly the kind of thing Maita originally exiled and quarantined you Immins for. You refuse to learn. Hasn't it ever occur-red to you the Immins are easily the most despised race in the entire galaxy only because you insist on doing these kinds of things? Are you so racially blind you can't see you're the only race who acts in such a manner? What's the matter with you?!"

"The Immin race has been in space for many thousands of years!" Cape screamed. "We've been refused our rightful place in the galaxy! We were in space thousands of years before you Swaz were even out of the slime! We want what is our right!"

"You've been in space for thousands of years only because the Maitans tried to help you," Tab replied. "Look what that got for them! In those same tens of thousands of years your reputation hasn't changed one least bit for the better. You will always be fighting among yourselves and are even doing it now on the one world the emperor – against the advice of myself and his advisers – has given back to you.

"You always interfere with emerging cultures when it would be a lot easier and safer to use unoccupied worlds for your silly schemes. You've been involved in every major crooked scheme in the empire and out for all those thousands of years. Without fail.

"There are empire ships waiting for you in orbit. You'll be blasted to atoms if you try to leave and you'll be blasted to atoms if you try to stay. You're dead contagion right now. You just haven't been buried yet."

"*You're* dead right now!" Xut yelled and shot him full in the face with the laser.

"Surprise! I'm shielded!" Tab said. "You're not!"

He shot her full in the face with a pencil laser. She fell at his feet.

"Next?" he said.

"What choice do we have?" Cape whined. "You said we'll all be killed if we leave or if we stay!"

"That's your problem," Tab replied. "It's exactly the choice you gave the people of this world. It's something you've brought on yourselves.

"I'm going back to Lopar's kingdom. I don't want to have to watch you die."

He turned and walked away, fully expecting to be shot in the back, though that wouldn't harm him.

"Are there other ships on the planet, TR?" he asked.

"I don't know. You go back to Lopar and finish setting up your system while I fine-scan the planet. I'll try to detect the power sources of any other ships. It should give you time."

There was a tremendous flash behind him.

"I sort of dropped a fusion grenade right into the door of that dome," TR reported. "The port to the ship was still open so there ain't nothing surviving in there."

"Send servos to dispose of their ship and see nothing's left around," Tab replied, climbed aboard his floater to head back to Lopar's kingdom, then changed his mind. He shouldn't return so soon, so he went to TR for the next two days.

He came back to the castle an hour after dark, walking along River Road. He stopped at Wooler's for a beer and to catch up on what was happening.

"We tried to stop you when you left," Wooler said. "We seen Feltron leave a piece back 'n didn't know if you was expecting 'im to spy er worse."

"Thank you, my friends," Tab replied. "I think Feltron is lost somewhere in the mountains. He won't find his way back here for at least ten years if ever.

"I see we're back to regular tableware?"

"Yuh! We done give Lopar most'a the gold," he said. "We're gonna have a tradesmen's club an' he's gonna build us all that water stuff and that kinda thing."

"I think maybe he's not so bad after all," Tab said. "You said that all along."

"Yuh, he ain't so bad. It's *her*!" he replied disgustedly.

He went from Wooler's to the castle. He entered the dining hall as the palace people were taking their seats. Lolu, who was the first to see him, squealed and ran to him, almost knocking him down.

He talked to Lopar during the meal and found the king had sent the largest ship with ample gold to buy and bring back the pipe and any books they could find.

"I'll make the rest of the gold this evening," Tab sug-gested. "I think I have enough frobishery bloofle. There won't be anymore for seven years so it'll have to do."

They discussed several new things and Lopar said he'd been given an idea by something Tab said and wanted to show him some sketches. Tab agreed and Lopar sent a page boy for the drawings.

Lopar had designed a jet boat that used pumps run by steam engines! It would work, but would need some modification.

"I used your pump in the river and can see how strongly the outlet moves when placed in the water," Lopar said. "Do you feel the fire nozzles will speed the water up?

"I saw these steam-driven motors in one of my books and have been studying it since you left. I'm sure it will work."

"I was going to suggest it," Tab replied. "I see your design is somewhat better than mine. That's good. I like the idea of the swivels on the nozzles. That should im-prove the steering over the rudder I planned. Perhaps we can use both that turn on the same device."

It seemed Lopar had a very good mind. This was the first real incentive he ever had to use it. He was going to become one of the scientists here!

Tab then went to his shower with Lolu and retired a bit early. He enjoyed the intimacy with her and was convin-cingly like a man who had been away for awhile.

In the morning he had the soldiers dispose of some of the lead, saying he could only make four more tons, which should be enough.

The largest part of the day was spent with Lopar and the boat design. Lopar was having a hull built to house the engine. It would be ready in about ten days. The boat would be fairly small, but would be very fast for the time. It could be utilized in the calmer seasons to bring books, furniture and fixtures. Tab hoped the speedier travel would also bring scholars and vacationers to bolster the economy. They would finance future expansions, too.

Lopar was turning out to be more than Tab thought possible. The stone cutters were carving the rock for the new buildings to be built. They would be completed in about three years.

"You mentioned making a patents court here," Lopar said. "I read about these patents in my library and can envision a safe system that is worldwide and respected. Prolly stated that some such centralized system would be needed as the world becomes more industrialized. Gloxim suggests an international court. They are both known authorities on business and have been trying to get a patent process in place to stimulate production of new ideas. They have called often and again for a centralized office of patents so one may know if he is working on a project already invented.

"Everything would have to be placed in a special cate-gory for crossreference. I think this will be a good place for the patent registry and the international trade court.

"I don't wish to sound too ambitious or to move too fast. This will take time and I will want progeny to complete those projects I start. That means I will be the first king in this kingdom ever to divorce, but Keenu is *not* going to mother any children of mine if I have a say in the matter! I will want someone who is fully qualified as an honorable woman. There is little chance Lolu will leave you for me, but I feel she is eminently qualified.

"I like your cook and there is no call for a king to marry royalty as in the old times. Would that there were! I would *not* be married to Keenu!

"Mima has no social graces, but she is strong and honor-able and is a striking woman. She will make a fine mother, but would she have me?"

"Mima has everything any man could ever reasonably want in a wife and mother," Tab said. "If you let her get away simply because she speaks like most people here you're a fool! Think how much closer to the people you'd be if you married her. They'd rally behind you more than they do now.

"I've seen the way you look at Mima. I know you'd prefer her to Lolu – the question being whether she would marry you. I don't know if she'd be happy as a queen."

"I don't need or want any damned queen!" Lopar cried. *"Keenu* is *that*! Look what she is! I need a wife for me and a mother for my children!"

"You'll have to discover a way," Tab replied. "I have an idea about the patent system that would perhaps deserve a patent for itself.

"Do you know much math?"

"I have read many of my books and fully know addition and subtraction, multiplication and division – and even fractions!" Lopar said proudly. "I even was able to teach myself a little formula math such as basic algebra and plane geometry!"

"That's very good," Tab said. "Do you know anything about binomials?"

"No," Lopar replied.

"My idea is to make a long box. Two of them. We can put cards of an exact size into," Tab said. "The cards will have holes and slots across the top in certain positions. There can be twelve or fifteen or as many as we ever need.

The holes will be in certain patterns, as will the slots, so it will make no difference which order the cards are placed in the box. Each card will have a pattern of holes and slots that no other card has. The category of any invention will be a binomial number. We'll have thin metal rods that will go through the holes in the box, aligned with the holes in the cards from one end to the other through the cards. The binomial number will be `written' on the cards using the holes and slots. If you run the rods through the holes in the proper pattern and lift them only the card with a particular number will remain in the box!"

"There will be many more categories than twelve or fifteen," Lopar argued. "We have to use a system that will allow use of thousands of cards!"

"No!" Tab argued. "Fifteen holes will let you use more than thirty two thousand different cards. Adding one more hole lets you double that. Each added hole doubles the number of the last one."

Tab showed Lopar how the system worked to where twenty holes used more than a million cards, no two of which would be alike. Lopar understood using zero as a place keeper so Tab explained that $1 = 1$, $10 = 2$, $11 = 3$, $100 = 4$, $101 = 5$, etc. Lopar worked it out to twenty places himself and was amazed.

The idea of making the boxes to hold up to five thousand cards would make one box per broad category and everything could be cataloged in very little space – and anyone could find any card in very short time, no matter how the cards were mixed.

The card would carry short descriptions, dates, patent numbers – which would be the binomial system number itself! – inventor and dates. It would have a unique file number to make further research efficient and fast.

If the rods were run through one at the time and those cards picked up placed in the side box by the time one ran the entire digital number only one card would remain and it didn't matter what order they ended up in the second box. The first box then became the second box for the next search.

Tab brought the simple old computer idea up to see how Lopar's mind would react to the challenge of new infor-mation and systems. He was more than pleased with the test results. Lopar was a good analytical thinker. This project was actually going to work! Lopar would dump his nymphomaniac queen and was actually going to establish this!

Tab thought it would be a friendly gesture to help Lopar get rid of Keenu.

When Tab left the dining hall he signaled for Mima to come to the tower room. Lolu came along to ask what was happening.

"Would you like to marry Lopar?" he asked Lolu.

"Me? No!" she retorted. "It's too restricting. I don't want to be a queen."

"I think Mima would be a great queen," Tab continued. "Just because she'd be independent and would never act any different than she does now qualifies her."

"Except who's going to murder the pfimewe queen so Lopar can remarry?" Lolu asked.

"Nobody," Tab replied. "He's going to divorce her."

"A king can't divorce!" Lolu cried.

"Lopar's gonna divorce that pfimewe?" Mima asked as she came into the room. "I think Lolu's right. No king kin divorce. Ut's agin custom."

"He's the king," Tab said. "He's not about to stay married to the pfimewe, as you call her. If you werc a man, would you want her as mother to your children?"

"'Twouldn't surprise me none if he kilt her," Mima said. "He'd orter done ut years ago!

"'E ain't a bad man. Tain't 'is fault 'e got stuck uth 'er. They orta be a way 'e could dump 'er."

"Would you marry him if he divorces her?" Tab asked.

"*Me*?! 'E's a king! 'E wouldn't 'ave *me*!" Mima cried.

"He told me you were, in his own words, `a striking woman and a woman who would make a fine mother!'" Tab replied. "He wants a woman he can be proud of. He thinks you show more natural poise and culture than any-one else in the kingdom and you show taste and breeding when you dress up. You don't make a silly spectacle of yourself."

"But I couldn't be no queen!" Mima wailed. "I'd be ever so proud ta be 'is wife, but I ain't got no high edecation ta be no queen! I dunt talk right!"

"His exact words were, `Keenu is a queen and look what she is!'" Tab replied. "He wants a woman to take care of the castle, raise the children to take over when he's too old and be a wife he can be proud of as well as a close companion he cares for. He doesn't want some whore who's selfish and vain and he certainly doesn't want another sex-mad pfimewe!

"He would never even look at another woman if you were his wife."

"You mean 'e akshully said 'e wanted me?" Mima asked.

"He did!" Tab answered. "Act surprised if he asks you, but I wanted to give you time to think it over.

"For what it's worth, I think you'll be a great queen!"

"If I jest knew how ta ak an talk!" she wailed.

"I can be your lady in waiting!" Lolu cried. "I can teach you! It will be fun!"

"Would ye?" Mima asked "Me? Queen?

"I dunt know!"

"Well, think it over," Tab said. "Lopar's going to do away with all this court and audiences and such silliness and will concentrate on being a good king and in bringing prosperity to the kingdom."

"I have ta tell ya I ain't no virgin," Mima said. "A king's sposed ta marry a virgin."

"Only the first time," Tab replied. "Keenu was supposed to be a virgin when they married.

"Hah! Only if you forget every male within twenty kilometers of Kopett's castle!"

Both Mima and Lolu giggled.

"I'll akshully say 'yes' so fast 'is toes'll twist up!" Mima said. "Ya done promised ta teach me everthin' Lolu! I'll hold ya to ut!"

"I'll be there for you," Lolu promised. "Now I'll have to see if we can make it a double wedding."

"Wait a minute!" Tab yelled. "I've never said one word about marriage!"

"Of course not!" Lolu said with a giggle. "I don't want to get married either. Wooler is marrying Greak's sister. It would be a good idea to have a fiesta so everyone can have a good time. When a king marries it's customary in this kingdom for everyone who wishes to marry to become part of the ceremony. It ensures good health, fortune and healthy, smart children."

"Lopar wants strong healthy children," Tab said. "That's one of the reasons he feels Mima'll make the best wife for him and would be best for the kingdom. Her whole family's strong, goodlooking and intelligent. What more could a man ask for in the mother of his children? – other than having a good woman he can care for and trust. He's noticed Mima for a long while, but felt she was too good a woman to ask for a romp with.

"You're the perfect wife for him, Mima."

She giggled and left.

"What a smart political move!" Lolu cricd. "The whole king-dom will rally behind Lopar if he marries a commoner like Mima and she'll be a strong woman without inter-fering with his duties. How smart! Lopar has surprised me again – or was this your idea?"

"It was Lopar's," Tab said. "I do agree, though. Heartily.

"A shower and to bed, wench!"

In the morning Tab went to the kitchen early to find Lopar having some of the gincha brew and sweetcake and chatting with Mima. Mima smiled at Tab as he entered.

"I done give King Lopar some ginchy brew," she said. "I dint think you'd mind, 'im bein' ta king."

"That's fine, Mima," Tab answered. "He might like some of the amaranth bread next time you make any."

"I uz gonna aks ya if ya wanted ut fer ta midday," she agreed.

"Fine," Tab said. "Perhaps Lopar will join us at midday? How are things, Lopar?"

"I would speak with you on an important matter of state," Lopar replied.

"I gotta git some veggies," Mima said as she went toward the outer door. "Ya know where everthin's at, NN."

She went out.

"She's a born diplomat," Tab said. "What did you want with me?"

"I wish to get shed of Keenu in a way that will ensure the public is behind me," Lopar confided. "I can't just dump her. I am forbidden to divorce, but I can change that. My council will ratify anything along those lines or I'll make it public that every one of them has shared her bed.

"Do you see any way I may avoid all that mess?"

"Who's she spending the night with?" Tab asked.

"I have no idea," he answered. "Anyone who will sleep with her is my guess. She's not exactly selective, as you've undoubtably noted before now.

"I *must* be rid of her! If I must I will take a knife and cut her damned throat! I may not be able to legally divorce her, but there are plenty of precedents for a king killing such a wife!"

Lolu came into the room, smiled at Lopar and Tab and poured

some of the gincha. "She's in bed with Bishop Loupe right now," she reported. "I couldn't help but over-hear.

"You made a negative remark about Loupe in front of the dining hall crowd not long ago. It would be a good time to throw both of them out of the kingdom. Loupe's always preaching that a married person must sleep only with his legal mate. You can show him to be a fraud and her a common whore.

"I know it enrages me and I'm a liberal person!"

"Is she in her suite?" Tab asked.

"Where else?" Lolu asked, smirking at them.

Tab stood and said, "Lolu, King Lopar, shall we get perhaps two engineers and go to the queen's quarters to discuss putting a shower and lavatory there?"

Lopar was nervous, but stood to say, "That would be a good idea. My queen will need those luxuries, especially when she is raising my family.

"Come along, my official alchemist and inventor and his trusted assistant. I am sure your *official* assistant, Lolu, will wish to keep most careful notes on every least aspect of our work here, Sir Northram."

They went outside where Lopar called two engineers from the pipeline work and a page. They went as a group to the queen's tower. Lopar was nervous, but set his jaw firmly and led the way, explaining to the engineers they must design a way to place a pipeline to bring water from the roof tank to the chamber and must design a drain line from the castle to down river, the drain to run from the kitchen and the King's and Queen's chambers.

As they came to the door Lopar turned to tell the en-gineers the water room was to be in a small room that now had an old unused desk in it and absentmindedly reached behind himself to throw the door open wide.

Lolu threw a hand to her mouth, stared in shock into the room, squealed and ran out onto the landing. Lopar turned to see Keenu and Loupe in a twisted position he could have sworn only a professional acrobatic team could accomplish.

"Keenu! Loupe!" he shouted, loud enough to wake the entire castle.

Keenu was trying to pick the bedcovers from the floor to cover them and Loupe was trying to burrow under the pillows.

"This is the last pebble! This one breaks the cart!" Lopar roared. "You and your fop there have one hour to be beyond the limits of this kingdom! In exactly one hour I send the guard to find you! If you are in this kingdom you are both to be beheaded on the spot! If you ever return to this kingdom you are declared outlaws and are to be executed on the spot by any citizen. That citizen will then be appointed knight or lady to the court!

"You! Girl! The alchemist's assistant! You have pen and paper. Draw a decree right now! These, my engineers and my alchemist, will witness.

"Write this: I, King Lopar, having discovered Queen Keenu in the arms of another married man in the bed-chamber I have supplied for her use – that embrace one of perverted sexual nature – do hereby and now declare Queen Keenu is not my spouse. Any marriage performed between the two of us is taken as nonbinding and as having never taken place for the simple cause SHE has demonstrated such ceremony to be meaningless.

"Decreed: Any marriage involving Keenu of Kopett is null and void and never took place.

"Further decreed: Keenu of Kopett is hereby declared outlaw in Lopar.

"Further decreed: Bishop Loupe by his own actions is declared outlaw in Lopar. Loupe is also stripped of any office in state or church.

"Instructions: Keenu of Kopett may remove only articles of personal clothing, jewelry, one carriage and one mountbeast and must be without the limits of Lopar before midday this date. Ex-bishop Loupe may depend on the charity of said Keenu of Kopett and may remove nothing except the clothing in which he arrived in this chamber.

"Ex-bishop Loupe must also be without the limits of Lopar by midday this date.

"Neither Keenu of Kopett nor Loupe may ever again set foot in Lopar under penalty of death.

"So sworn and attested.

"Leave a line for my signature and have all here to sign the decree below my signature. I am a bachelor king and will actively seek a new queen worthy of the station who will raise the future rulers of Lopar and who will be morally acceptable to the people of Lopar – a queen who will be no embarrassment to myself or the citizens!

"This I swear.

"Put that as an addendum to the document, Lady Lolu."

Lolu was writing as fast as she could and called Lopar over to tell her some of it again, then everyone signed it. Lopar took the document and started down the stairwell, but turned back to yell, "Keenu! Pfimewe! You and that perverted fop have little time! Begone – or be dead! This is sworn! I will enter this document in the official court immediately.

"Engineers! We came to design a water room here. Con-tinue in that to prepare this chamber for the new queen.

"Alchemist, you and your assistant will accompany me to the court as witnesses in the entry of this document into records.

"Pfimewe and fop! Time grows ever the shorter! Begone or be dead!"

He turned and went down the stairs, followed by Lolu and Tab.

"That was brilliant, Lopar!" Lolu said when they were out of the hearing of the others. "To declare the marriage never took place means you aren't bound by the rule of no divorce!"

"I am king and can make new rules should I so choose," Lopar explained. "That was done so she could not claim anything at all. It is purely from charity on my part to allow her clothes and carriage, but I now have another little problem.

"As I wasn't married I can't marry anyone not a virgin and that rule I declare to be valid and will respect it fully!

"Write me another decree, Lady Lolu: I, King Lopar, do hereby decree that all women and girls employed in this castle in any manner at this time who are not married as of this date to be virgins.

"See how easy it is to make rules to fit the situation? You are a virgin until this evening when you share NN's bed again!"

"Golsamighty! Do we *have* to wait until this evening?" Lolu replied with a grin. "There's an old joke about a professional prostitute telling her girlfriend she was moving to another town to start over as a virgin. She could really have *done* it if she was here right now working as temporary kitchen help!"

They entered the decrees in the court records and listened to the court lawyers mumbling that it should have been done the day after the wedding when Keenu was already sleeping with the entire palace guard.

Lopar said he was distressed by all this turmoil and would go to his own chamber. He asked Lolu to please request that Mima bring a pot of hot gincha brew and amaranth bread for the midday meal to that chamber for him. He asked Lolu and Tab to forgive him for breaking the midday meal plans they had and to forgive Mima if she had other duties at that time.

Tab spent the rest of the day working with the engineers on various aspects of the water delivery system and with the wood craftsmen building a special boat ordered by Lopar. Lolu spent the entire afternoon with Mima, the two giggling and whispering together. Lopar, after seeing Loupe and Keenu out of the town from his balcony, worked with engineers building a library and luxury inn.

That evening when Tab and Lolu seated themselves at the king's table Lopar came in, nodded, and took his seat. Lolu seemed as excited as though she had a secret she was keeping from Tab so he acted like he had no idea what could be afoot.

A new girl came out with their food cart to serve Lopar with them. It was a repeat of their first meal Mima prepared and was equally good. Tab's analyzers told that him only Mima could have prepared the food. There were distinctive touches to the way she used the spices that couldn't be taught.

Lolu saw him looking perplexed and leaned to him to quietly whisper, "Mima wants to cook the food, but she feels she really shouldn't serve so her niece is doing that. She'll teach the girl everything."

Tab nodded and everything was normal until time for their dessert, which Mima brought in. She was dressed to perfection and looked every inch a glamorous queen. All eyes were on her as Lopar stood.

"My people! I have an announcement! As a bachelor king it is now incumbent upon me to choose a queen to give me progeny to carry on the duties of state for our kingdom when I can no longer properly perform those duties.

"I have made my choice and have asked the woman to consider the proposal.

"Before all of you, my people, I ask my chosen bride, Mima de Castile, if she will have me."

Mima drew herself up and looked nervously at the people in the room, then into Lopar's eyes.

"My Lord Lopar," she said clearly, "I am much honored and pledge my love and energies to you and the kingdom. I accept. Unreservedly!"

Lopar looked startled, then hugged her.

"I taught her what to say tonight!" Lolu whispered to Tab. "She practiced all afternoon! She did it perfectly!"

"I would have thought she couldn't speak without her dialect coming through," Tab said.

"I'm going to teach her one new thing every ten days," Lolu replied. "First is to stop dropping her `H'es. She'll never be really good, but that will help and people won't ever say she's trying to be more than she is."

"I think personally that she's far more than anyone gives her credit for being," Tab argued. "That woman has smarts to spare! She'll keep Lopar in line and he'll love it!"

A plush seat was brought and Mima sat next to Lopar. They conversed quietly until the last course was finished, then Lopar stood to announce the wedding would be held in fifteen days in the open courtyard. All who wished to be married at the ceremony could come the morning before to file the necessary papers.

"He's far more than I ever suspected or suspect yet," Tab said as he and Lolu went to bed. "His reactions were tempered much too far by the actions of Keenu. He'd given up hope of ever amounting to anything. Now he knows there's greatness in him and won't let it go. He'll be driven from now on. I think he'll accomplish a hell of a lot!"

As Tab was laying next to Lolu feigning sleep TR reported it had found another group of Immins. This time there were six of them in the same type of setup Feltron led them to.

"They're safe enough where they are right now," TR sent, "I'll keep three spy floaters there to watch every move and finish the survey with the others, then we can mop up and go.

"I think these are waiting for some kind of message from Xut and company and are getting nervous because they haven't heard anything. I think Xut was the leader. I wish we'd put her on the probe. I want to know how they got off Orta undetected!"

"I doubt they ever were on Orta," Tab replied. "They were on some planet – maybe one of those things where they were going to take over the empire that no one knew about – and came here to start the whole mess over again.

"I think there are four or five females there?"

"Five. One male," TR said.

"There'll be one other place where they have a lot of female breeders," Tab continued. "They'll want to start another Immin race here and build it until they're strong enough to take over the empire, then the galaxy, then the universe.

"They'd wipe each other out after a few years here. Trouble is they'd wipe out these people at the same time. That's the major problem with every one of these schemes. If it was only a matter of Immins killing off Immins I'd say to let them go.

"We do have to protect the innocent. That's the part of our reason for existing that will never change."

"Yo!" TR agreed. "They never change. You know exactly what you're gonna find before you find 'em."

In the morning Tab worked with the designers on the new water system. There was a deep sandy spit running through the center of town close behind the road all the shops and inns were on so they decided to bury the pipes two meters deep, encase them in solid concrete for the hot water, then cool water lines a meter to one side of the hot. They were in a semitropical zone so there would never be a problem with the pipes freezing. The sand would also insulate the pipes very well.

The boat was ready the following day. He worked all day to install the pump and the wood-fired steam engine he'd designed. The nozzles were on swivels with slip-joints so the boat could be turned with them if the rudder ever failed. They were angled very slightly inward to get the best thrust in straight movement.

In the evening he met with Lopar and the engineers to work out ways to accomplish various of their projects and to diagram a general plan/layout of where the theaters, restaurants and housing would be. They worked out many minor details and made lists of materials for Lopar to order. When the engineers left Tab and Lopar discussed how best to get the word out to the scholars and scientists they wanted to come.

"Tie it to the patenting process," Tab suggested. "Let it be known should a scientist or scholar have something patented or even the idea that leads to an advance he can apply to a special committee. If the committee decides his ideas have merit – and I don't mean things like turning lead to gold or making jewels – he'll be accepted here. The primary concentration will be about those things that advance the race, not things that will simply make someone a bit more wealthy. Medicine, transportation, communications, housing and to thwart criminality should be given first and by far the highest priority.

"You can select one committee for the arts and another for sciences. If an artist shows great promise he can be brought here for a fixed period of time during which he produces or he loses the grant."

"Yes!" Lopar agreed. "They must be able to produce something of value, but it may not be sold. They must prove their ability. Whatever they do here will be shared in fixed amount with the kingdom, the kingdom will in turn finance the work time.

"Some will fail so we must work on a realistic scale. The kingdom gets a fixed fraction of funds from all products made here to finance new research.

"What do you think of another system of patents for books and arts, such as symphonies? I'm sure you know how valuable books and art are. I have paid great amounts for some of my books. There should be a way!"

"Maybe some kind of certificate to the writer of a book, art or symphony saying the original document is in the library here and the author is the only one who may receive payment for the work," Tab replied. "Maybe a law establishing how many years the author is to receive a fixed fraction or amount for all sales of copies of the work and *very* strong penalties against anyone who copies the work for sale without contract with the author.

"It could be done. Those are things for the future. We have to finish some of the things we've started first!"

"Oh, but I have so many ideas and only my one life!" Lopar cried. "It will take to the fifth generation to do it all!"

"That's why you'll have to spend time with your wife to be!" Tab pointed out with a grin. "Otherwise there won't be a fifth generation to do it. There won't be a second."

They chatted awhile and went their separate ways. Early the following morning the boat was tested. It worked a bit better than he thought.

He and Lopar, along with the man who designed and built the boat and the two who built the steam engine, went perhaps ten kilometers up the coast and back again. They had a compass so could find their way easily.

"We have to find a more efficient fuel," Tab insisted. "What with all the fresh water we have to carry for the steam wood's much too heavy and bulky."

"In Work City they have iron tanks lined inside with copper they can compress the natural gas that comes from the vents in the mines into," Tall, the head engineer who built the engine said. "They use it to cook and to melt their ores to make the iron for molding into pipe. There's no reason we couldn't use the tanks to run our engines. We just have to find a way to control the pressure.

"They have what they call regulators, but they won't tell anyone how they work. The pressure in the tanks is so high the gas is liquid so it has to be controlled."

"I could invent a regulator, I think," Tab said. "We could force the gas through very small holes into a chamber under the steam generator. Make a way for air to get in and the smoke to get out and we have it.

"It will take some thought."

He worked the whole afternoon to make a very complicated set of springs and diaphragms to control gas flow. He wanted to make it primitive and difficult enough to where someone would design a simple regulator.

He then helped install some pipes from the roof tank into what would be the queen's chambers, though Mima made it plain that she intended to stay in the same bedchamber with her husband, which pleased Lopar.

The next night TR announced it had located the rest of the Immins parked in the desert on the opposite side of the world under very good camouflage cover. The scans were complete and there were only the two camps of them.

In the morning Tab told Lopar and Lolu he had to go away, but would try to return before the wedding.

Lolu asked if his whole life was running away all the time.

"That's part of being an alchemist," Tab replied. "I seldom stay anywhere as long as I've stayed here."

She nodded and said, "Then you'll not be too hurt if I marry someone else at the ceremony?"

"I've said from the first I had no intention of ever marrying anyone," Tab said. "I didn't know you had a mate selected."

"Yes. Captain Greak has asked me to marry him many times," she replied. "I think he'll be very pleased if I say yes – and the ceremonies are beautiful! A girl dreams of being married at the Royal Wedding Ceremony!"

"If I'm not back by then I wish you happiness," Tab said.

He knew the customs here would make her an excellent wife to Greak. Both partners could have as many lovers as they pleased before marriage. Once married you were married. Period.

Half an hour later he headed for TR.

Chapter three

"Okay, TR," Tab remarked as he entered the hold. "Let's get this show on the road, as Z would say.

"Gimme some kinda rundown. What've we got? Where are they and how vulnerable? How far from anyone or anything they can screw up for the next thousand years – because we both know that given any chance whatever they will."

"Two camps," TR replied. "One in the mountains, a survey ship. Type F-two, like Xut had. Got the same kind of dome and is as far from any native populations. Six persons aboard.

"You know about them. Same setup all the way around.

"Number two's on the desert half a planet away. There are a total of one hundred fifty plus Immins there. Thirty or so males for breeders. The females are always in charge of these groups with the males selected to breed a new race.

"If they'd breed something new it wouldn't be so bad. They always end up breeding more Immins.

"Gonna take the mountains first?"

"Yeah. Let's get on with it," Tab agreed. "I just want to be rid of Immins! It can't be quick enough to suit me!"

TR moved to where it was just out of sight-range from the coast, went high enough to go over the rough mountain range to the south and west of Lopar and went in low to follow a long deep valley for a distance. When TR settled on a ledge it said, "They're about half a kilometer around to the left on a ledge much like this one. I thought I'd stop here and we'd try to get one of them on the probe.

"I'm not as advanced as Maita in using the floater probes so you'll have to help with that. Maita is going to install the better control system, but we haven't had the time.

"I think these will be the bigshots and the ones on the colony ship breeders. Higher-up Immins don't like being around their own kind – for which I don't blame them.

"What do you want to do? Fly in, disable them and put one on the probe?"

"We're not in that much of a hurry. They could get a message out if we go in without totally wiping them out so we'll take them by surprise," Tab said slowly. "They're expecting a message from Xut so I'll deliver a message from Xut. That way we can get the most important one there on the probe."

"Cripes! They aren't going to let you walk in there like an expected guest!" TR snapped.

"I'm a magician, remember?" Tab said smugly. "These Immins will fall for anything like that crap. They're superstitious as all hell! Remember how fast Xut's bunch fell for the magic stuff you handed them on the videos.

"I'll need the shield again with a probe added and some mumbo-jumbo crap.

"Carry a video circuit concealed in some jewelry and a high light source – something they can't find if they examine the shield."

"I'll hang a bunch of thin magnesium strips that'll give you intense colored lights and smoke to form runes. It'll be on a frame in front of the shield that'll totally vaporize. It won't hurt the shield in any way and won't leave a trace," TR suggested.

"Now, was that so hard?" Tab asked.

"Stick it in your ear!" Tab snapped.

Tab worked on the special clothing to conceal several devices while TR worked on the shield/ floater/probe. Tab waited until everything tested out perfectly, then took the shield to walk casually around the mountain. He was able to approach the ship closely without being seen.

Two Immins were at the dome entrance under the awning and two more were moving around the far side of the ledge.

"Get a small floater directly across from here and have it make some sort of sound that'll get their attention," Tab sent.

"Yo!" TR replied.

Tab waited a couple of minutes more, then started to feel a slightly disturbing sensation that wasn't quite pleasant, nor was it obvious. Almost subliminal. It built quickly, became much more unpleasant and became directed to the far side of the ledge. The Immins were running out to stare across at the far side of the ledge. Tab moved out until he was close behind them. The small floater suddenly appeared and moved in a streak of intense light to him. He pushed the fuse for the magnesium. The small floater soared away hidden in the glare from the magnesium flares.

The light suddenly went out and there were lazy swirls of brightly colored smoke rising to reveal Tab standing there. The Immins ran toward him, stopped, turned away, then ran toward him again, shielding their eyes (That must be giving them trouble if they stared directly at that magnesium glare!). Three of them had drawn weapons.

"Who are you?" one female screamed at him.

"I am Sir Northram, at your service," he said, bowing with a flourish. "I have brought a message from one called Xut in the mountains of the Kingdom of Lopar."

"I'm Zeef," the female answered. "What's the message? I never heard of any kingdom of Lopar, but I haven't heard of much of anything from Xut."

"It is not for you," Tab said and stood silently.

"Well? Who's it for?" she asked.

"The proper person will reveal herself," Tab replied.

"I'm Code," the male said.

Tab stared him in the eyes and refused to speak.

"Listen, scum!" Code yelled, waving his heat laser. "You know what this is?"

"It is a silly little weapon that has no effect on a wizard of my caliber," Tab replied haughtily. "Should you be so stupid as to use it I will turn the heat beam back upon you and you will be as dead as one called Cape, who tried the same silly foolishness. Had you any intelligence at all you would realize the message *could not* be delivered should you be so foolish as to use such a weapon – and should I be unable to turn the beam. Cape was stupid. *You* are stupid."

Another female stepped forward and asked, "Cape is dead?

"Please come with me to the privacy of the, uh, place over here."

Tab stared in her eyes for a moment, then said, "It is merely a vessel that travels among the stars." He didn't move.

"I'm called Quirt," she introduced. "Please come inside where we'll have privacy and tell me what Xut sent for me. I know she would send a message to no other."

Tab nodded and went before her to the dome and inside.

"How do you travel?" she asked as she directed him to an office in the belly of the craft.

"The mind has many great abilities if properly trained," he answered as he slipped the anesthetic gun into his hand. The shield pulsed a slight vibration and he looked at the video telling him there were audio and video devices around the room. Quirt didn't pay any attention to the shield.

"Are you telekinetic?" she asked.

"I use the powers of the mind to move myself and many other things," Tab replied. "I was near this place in the past and knew of it when Xut described it. That is not important."

The floater noted it had located the various audio and video pickups and Tab had it knock them out.

"I have blinded all the devices watching and listening to us," Tab said calmly. "The message is for you alone..."

He shot her with the instant anesthetic, quickly put her on the probe, waited until the signal said the probe was finished, took the exact position he was in when he shot her, then waited until the green dot on the floater turned orange to indicate the antidote was fired.

"... it is this – and you are to act with alacrity and care," he said.

He seemed to go into a kind of trance and his voice became a monotone.

"I quote Xut: You will not broadcast any radiation-detectable transmissions for any reason. The empire has a ship in orbit and is seeking us out. There has been a traitor. They will fire on us without preamble should they find us. Use no detectable power. Keep a low profile and stay under camouflage at all times. Do *not*, repeat, do *not* use communications. I will be in contact when it is safe. End of message."

He dropped back into a `normal' voice. "I will go now. If you wish to return a message tell me and I will carry it. I will first go to the desert ship. I can carry a message to either Xut or the other ship or both."

"No!" she cried. "No message! We have to institute security precautions! Go!"

Tab strolled casually out, walked to the edge of the ledge and right off the end. He fell across the floater, which raced him off among the trees below. When the Immins reached the steep ledge they heard the strange subliminal sounds and saw a flash shooting off to the east.

Tab reached TR and was standing inside in less than five minutes.

"What now?" TR asked.

"Process the probe read," Tab replied. "If we have what we need we'll be an empire ship coming in to find them. If they fire at us we shoot back."

"Yo!" TR said. "Here's what we have from the probe.

"They were en route to Brenct with another load of colonists and diverted them when the fireworks started in the roundup eight years ago. They visited two very close planets, Warnn and Plebus, but settled on this one because they didn't think the others were advanced enough to do them any good. This planet had some early iron age industrialization, but not much population. They planned to use their technology to garner economic control of the world. They would then use the natives here as slave labor until they had established a viable colony, then would wipe the natives out and use their technological base to build a war force to strike at the empire.

"Xut was head of the whole plan, but Quirt would be in the perfect position to assassinate her and take over herself, thus becoming empress of the Maitan Empire and soon – queen of the universe!

"They never learn."

They waited a few minutes longer, then flew in close around the mountain. The Immin ship fired as soon as they were spotted. TR left a bubbling crater where they had been.

"Well, might as well head for the desert!" TR suggested.

They were soon hovering above a large cargo ship that had been converted to a colony ship. "Immins!" TR radioed "We are from the Maitan Empire! You are under arrest! Any resistance and you will be wiped from the face of this planet without hesitation!"

There was a short pause, then the radio popped.

"Attention empire ship! We are not armed! I repeat, we are not an armed ship! We will follow your instructions. Do not fire on us! We are not armed!"

"What are they trying to pull?" Tab said. "They damned well *are* armed!"

"Let's wait," TR suggested. "They have some fabulous plan I'm sure."

They waited a few moments, then TR sent, "Gather everyone and all supplies inside of your ship. We will escort you to Orta and disable the ship after you land there. Any least resistance or noncompliance with our orders and you will be destroyed. You are illegally aground on a contact restricted planet and we are under no obligation to warn you before destroying you. Beware!"

They waited for over three hours, then the ship radioed it was prepared to take off.

"Rise above the atmosphere and await orders before going into IDmode drive," TR radioed back. "Make no least move without instructions."

"They plan to drop and snake us, eh?" Tab said.

"I'll let them know that's impossible as soon as they're in space," TR answered.

They rose with the ship until they were above air.

"Before you do anything stupid, we placed a gravity grapple identification tracer on your ship with a floater as you rose above atmosphere," TR radioed. "Should you attempt to drop and snake in IDmode it won't work. Set your moder at TTH one. Two four five, minus one, twenty eight eight ninety two and await drop-in signal."

There was silence for a moment, then TR said, "Better brace yourself. They've set a hell of an energy source at ready so they're gonna try to shoot us down or something. They've figured we're the only ship out here and they can shoot us down and jump."

"They can't shoot and jump at the same time!" Tab replied. "That could dephase their moder!"

"Immins were never educated in military matters," TR replied dryly. "They were enough trouble without it."

"Can you warn them?" Tab asked.

"Huh! They won't listen, but I'll try," TR answered. "Hear me, Immins! Do *not* attempt to...."

TR was rocked by a sudden shock, then there was an intense multicolored flash that flickered a few times, then even TR was thrown around and Tab was damaged quite a bit. When he regained consciousness servos were busily reconstructing parts of him.

"I take it they dephased?" Tab asked.

"Welcome back to the existing," TR answered. "I'm glad they were far enough from the planet that no one was hurt there."

"I'm glad they weren't closer to *any* matter source or they might have caused an unbelievable disaster in two planes!" Tab replied. "Do you think I'll be put back together in time to go to the wedding?"

"You're going back there?" TR asked. "I think we can make it. I have to make a few parts, but the idea of putting the brain in a foam padding saved you. "I wish my architect was as good as Maita's. I could have you done in a couple of hours. As it is it'll take several days. Do you have any idea how ridiculously complicated those secon-dary circuits are?"

"Maita used only the finest handcrafted – well, that good, anyhow – parts on me," Tab replied haughtily. "This is rather unpleasant. Do you mind if I turn off until you're finished?"

"Go for it!" TR said.

Next thing Tab knew TR was saying, "Get up! You can't stay there forever! You are the laziest one machine I have ever seen – and I've seen a hell of a lot of machines!"

"Blow it out your exteriors, Gas Brain!" Tab snapped. "Damn! It's good to be back!"

"Okay! Let's go to a wedding," TR said. "It's day after tomor-row."

They went into the ocean and Tab was soon on River Road on his way to Lopar's castle. There were already hundreds of people gathered, but he was shown to a private table as soon as he was seen entering the pub. Greak and Wooler came to greet him.

"I never thought we'd get any kinda magician we'd like, but you done spun this place round!" Greak greeted. "Lolu said you knowed she was gonna marry me. She said you done give your good fortunes ta us an I 'preciate it.

"I knows she's too good fer me, but we could make it work."

"I know you'll make her a good husband and she'll make you a good wife," Tab said. "I hear Wooler's marrying your sister. I wish you two the very best, too."

He stayed at Wooler's for more than an hour, then headed for the castle where there were so many people he almost couldn't force his way through. Mima was with Lolu on the palace entrance platform giving advice to those about to be married. She saw Tab and called, "Let that man through! He's the one Lopar's having be his first brother! Let 'im – I mean let him through!"

Tab jumped to the platform to hug both Mima and Lolu. "I see you're saying your `h'es," Tab said. "You really do seem to have the love and respect of the people around here. I'll bet Lopar's so proud he doesn't know what to do!"

"Yup! He looks like he's going to pop at times," Lolu replied. "I'll take you in and you can find him somewhere. Probably in your tower. He goes there because he made it a standing order no one else is to go there so he can work alone on some of his projects.

"You said he'd be a driven man and you were right! He invented a better thing for the gas tanks, what he calls a regulator valve thing. It's simple and works better than yours. He says you always were happy when someone else improves your things.

"He says we'll get our own gas from near the tar pits to the south if we drill like they do at Work City because that's how they found theirs. He read it in one of his books. He has an idea to pipe the gas right into peoples' kitchens for the cooking and to heat water. He says there's a thing on his regulator, a spring, that can have heat bend it or something so the fire will go out by itself when the water's hot or something.

"He has hundreds of ideas. We stopped trying to keep up. You can hear all that from him.

"I can't stay with you anymore. I consider I'm the same as

married since I told Greak yes. I hope you understand."

"I certainly do!" Tab said. "I was talking to Greak on my way here and he's very excited. He'll make a good husband for you. You go back to Mima now. You're really making a lady out of her!"

Lolu giggled and went back out as Tab went up the stairs. He entered the top tower room to find Lopar there working with his neon tube light. It would spark, but wouldn't start the plasma flow to sustain a steady light.

"I think you'll have to make a two-way coil to send a long arc through after we start the mercury vaporization," Tab suggested.

Lopar whirled and grabbed him in a bear hug.

"I was afraid you'd never return here!" he cried. "I made you first brother at the wedding on hope!

"Have you seen Mima? She's learning to talk without the accent she had! I'm so proud of her!

"Lolu is marrying Greak. He's the captain of the town guard. Good man. Stubborn as anyone, but smart and fair at the same time.

"What do you mean about the light? I found all your notes. I hope you don't mind my working on these things. I wasn't sure you would return."

"I can't stay after the wedding," Tab replied. "I wanted to tell you there are some little ideas in the notes you might want to work on. That's what I wrote them down for.

"We can make the light work by putting the current through a coil and capacitor with a thing like a spring to cause the coil to charge and discharge rapidly. That'll increase the arc and the gas will glow.

"I think you can let the current drop again once the gas is glowing – according to the book in your library.

"They could have made a good light years ago in Work City if anybody'd thought of coating the tube with the phosphors."

They worked all night on the light until the king was able to say the electric light was proven.

Lopar dreamed of making some kind of large generator and sort of "piping" electricity for lights into all the houses in the town! People could come into a room, push a switch to deliver electricity to the light, then hold the button down for about fifteen seconds to start the coil. The light would continue to glow until the electricity was switched off!

Water, gas and electric lights – all in everyone's house!

Yes, this kingdom was going to teach the whole world how to live in ease and luxury!

The wedding was a huge success. The new king and queen rode up and down the river in the new steam- driven boat. Lolu, Wooler, Greak and Anna, Wooler's new wife, sat in the pavilion and gave bawdy advice to the newly-weds.

Next day Tab gave Lopar the map of the nearby island where the gincha and other exotic plants were growing so he could keep a supply on hand. The kingdom was also going to give Klemmr some new gourmet foods!

The following day Tab said his goodbyes and left, walking along River Road.

"Damn it all, TR! Why do I always get so involved with these organics? I hate to leave here!" Tab said. "I'll miss them all. I never fail to be surprised at how changeable some of them are. I wouldn't have given you a bet of a credit against a fortune that Lopar would ever amount to anything when I first got here. Now he's going to be a hero for all time on this world.

"Mima was a kitchen maid, now she's queen.

"I think Lolu's the only one of the whole bunch at that castle who didn't change one bit. I'll actually miss her the most. I *do* like this sex stuff.

"I could become a male Keenu – and I don't like that idea one little bit!"

"Have Maita retune you down some," TR replied. "We'll be home on EC in a couple hours. Another smashing success by the DeSixtee Detective Agency!"

"Go to Neeahna before going home," Tab suggested. "I want to report to Louahna."

"Yo!" TR said.

They went directly to Neeahna to spend almost a day with Louahna and Heleemius, who came to hear about the world and what Tab had done. After that they went to EC where they were debriefed by Maita, who wanted every slightest detail where any Immins were concerned.

TR was in its cave hangar where servos would go over every single circuit and device carefully. Tab would go in for his own checkup after visiting with everyone on EC.

Ape wanted him to go to Ape's World to see how things were going. Ape was very old now, but had become a close friend so Tab stepped into the transmat to spend four days at Ape's new home on the planoformed world, then stepped back into the Ape's World transmat to appear on Z's terrace. Thing was working on its gardens under the nearby sea. Z was on the mountain planting some new orchids.

Tab sat on the terrace to wait for them to come back in. He held long silent conversations with Maita and TR while he waited, Maita telling all about the Freenz ship and TR telling some about Klemmr and Lopar.

I'll improve the atomic architect in TR while it's here for service. It's a better model than the one I always used, but will need calibration. We'll have the time now. I'm adding a few other little ideas as we go. I'm impressed with this Lopar and feel he'll accomplish some important things. I also feel you give too much of yourself and you'll be hurt. Such people come along in many cultures and do these great things. Those things are almost always lost in short time. Great cities with large libraries who cater to the arts and sciences last for a few years, then are lost or destroyed.

"This one invented the electric light," Tab said. "That'll make a difference."

Only in that his name will be remembered, but nothing will change – which isn't reason for despair. You've given them a much brighter time in a rather brutal and bloody part of their history than they would have had. Perhaps you've taken them past certain of the worst things. Your reason for being there was to find the intrusive force affecting them from outside and you did that. I was so angered when TR told me there were Immins on that world I didn't trust my own actions had I gone. Will we ever be free of them?

"It really doesn't look like it," Tab replied. "Every time we think we've made any progress against them we find another bunch doing exactly the same sordid things. It sometimes leads to interesting work for us, but their only aim is to become Queen Empress of the Universe and other places."

They'll never learn. I'm ashamed to say I'll be glad when they're extinct! They'll soon have Orta burned to lifelessness.

"Here comes Z," Tab said.

The light from the yellow sun was rising across the ocean, casting a brilliant gold tip to the waves to mingle with the red from behind. Z came down the mountain with his arms loaded with assorted plants and didn't see Tab sitting on the lip of the pool by the entrance to his home. He spread the plants on the marble floor of the terrace and sorted them according to what altitude he felt was most likely to help them thrive on this new world. Tab said nothing for almost an hour until Thing came riding its floater from the ocean where it had been working in its gardens – the difference being that Thing's gardens were as much as two kilometers deep under the ocean.

[Hello, Tab. You look bored.]

Z looked up to see Tab for the first time. "How long have you been there?" Z asked.

"A couple of hours," Tab answered. "I was watching you sort out the plants. You seemed absorbed and I hated to distract you."

We want to all be together to hear about your big adventure. I told them nothing.

[Maita hasn't told us anything yet, but it's been ranting and swearing so much we knew you must have found a new Pweetoo brood somewhere, minimum. We hope so at least. We'd really hate to think that Maita was going to stay that way.]

"Maita's only been impossible for a couple weeks so we were able to stand it," Z agreed. "Let me finish and we'll all get something to eat and talk about what we've been up to. I know you didn't find any Pweetoos or Maita would have been gone!"

Tab and TR could handle the problem. I was already in the air as soon as I heard about it! TR talked me into coming back here and letting them do their job.

"Now I *am* curious!" Z exclaimed. "This'll only take another few minutes. Thing, get us some food ready. Tab can have a nice can of oil or something."

"I should have brought the wife back with me!" Tab said. "You wouldn't make that kind of joke around her!"

"Wife?"

Wife?

[Wife?]

Tab grinned and went inside to wait for Z to finish sorting his plants. Thing gathered the meal from the synthesizer and had it set out when Z came in. They all sat around the table to eat and talk.

"Okay!" Z finally said. "Tell us all about it!"

"I went to a planet called Klemmr where Louahna dis-covered there was a problem," Tab related. "I stayed at the royal palace there where I met this girl.

"We had a wonderful time.

"There was a mass wedding, as is their custom when the king got married. My girl and about sixty others got married at the ceremony.

"It's tradition, you see. All the girls want their wedding to be at the king's ceremony because it's good luck and your kids will be healthy and smart.

"That's about it.

"Oh, yeah! The Immin thing came up so TR and I had to check on that. That took a couple of days and it got a little rough at the end, but TR put me back together pretty well.

"What about the Freenz ship? I want to hear all about that! TR and I will go to Freenz as soon as our overhauls are finished."

[*Immins*?! Surely you're joking?]

"Immins?!" Z cried. "So *that's* what was wrong with Maita! No wonder it was acting like that!"

Forget about the damned Immins! What about that girl! Did you marry that girl?!

"I merely said `the wife' and that my girl got married," Tab replied innocently. "I left before the holiday was over."

You were living with her! So who did she marry? Royalty?

"Captain Greak from the palace guard," Tab replied. "He'd asked her a number of times and she wanted to get married at the festival so she ... did."

[Are you going to tell us all about this or are we going to have to dismantle you and take the memory chips?]

"I have but recently been rebuilt because that moder dephased and messed me up!" Tab replied haughtily. "I don't care to be taken apart again!"

[Moder dephase? And you're still around?]

TR told me about that. Do you want to tell them about your little adventure?

"I brought a crystal for Z and you can send to Thing now," Tab said. "TR will fill you in on the wedding and stuff like that."

Z placed the crystal and Thing was quiet for ten minutes while Maita "sent" the full experience to it.

[We have to seek out any more patches of these Immins and stamp them out! You shouldn't have even considered taking them to Orta. You know that! They are outlaw and had even landed on a restricted world!]

Orta's in the middle of a nuclear world war. The Immins will be extinct there in a matter of days. I've sent the entire empire fleet to do close sensor scans of every planet they can reach for Immins. I've invented a new sensor that can detect any ship that has a power sphere on a world. I'm having them placed on trader ships so they can help. If they get a scan they call Fleet.

[There are more than two billion possible planets they can use. It's hopeless.]

"Our best hope is contact with Louahna and Heleemius. Those people will find them for us best, but we're never going to stop looking," Tab said. "They've had thousands of years to establish little hidden colonies all over the galaxy.

"I sincerely hope we can consider the problem as solved now, but we can't be smug about it or we'll really find ourselves in a tight spot someday.

"We have to stop them *before* they screw up any more worlds!

"Have you seen Ape lately?"

[We were on Ape's World a few days ago for him to show us around the place. I'm so glad he lived to see his dreams come true. He's got a fine family and has built a whole world for himself. He's very old. He knows he'll die soon.]

"I'll really miss him," Z agreed. "I think I'm the only one who really understood him and I know he's the only one of the original group who understood me."

[I understand you! Too well!]

"You only think you do!" Z retorted.

They started playing the game and were still at it hours later. Everyone could relax now and enjoy the pleasures of the magnificent world.

Z spent the next thirty seven days with his plants while Thing contoured a whole new section of its undersea garden and planted it with some of the recently-acquired lifeforms. Maita developed a method to project the scenes from the gardens into the holovid on Z's wall. The effect was so real one could almost feel the currents as they swept through the colorful forms.

TR was completely rebuilt with a number of new devices both it and Maita designed while Tab had the new streng-theners built into his basic frame to prevent his being broken up again as he so recently had been. The brain protection, a special plastic foam, was checked and found to be more than ample for the job.

A few Immin encampments were found. Fleet handled most of them quickly. Rollo was in charge of that segment of Fleet and gave orders that action against any Immin anywhere in the galaxy was to be taken immediately upon their discovery and that the report he wanted to relay to the emperor was that the problem *had been* located, assessed and solved within minutes.

The group played their regular games and tricks on one another, kept working on their personal projects and visited around worlds like Ape's World, Zeena, Parf and New Zule – and Freenz. There was a rare respite from serious trouble for a little while.

It was more than two years since the last of the Immins were found and removed by Rollo. Very little had hap-pened that was of any consequence to the crew except that Tab did a couple more things for Louahna and others. They were almost entirely what were once called the "legwork" jobs of detection and were resolved with little fanfare.

Maita renovated certain empire functions, TRD-60 had some new things added to its workings, as did Maita. The two developed a better set of equations for TTH14 and were slowly refining their use of the plane.

Thing added a new section to its gardens and Z was using a special device invented by Maita to make "photographs" of the orchids. The "pictures" looked, felt, smelled and tasted like the real flowers, but were just small silvery balls until placed in the projector.

He was making a classification system that could iden-tify any plant from any explored planet in the galaxy (So long as it was studied and placed in the catalog computer). They'd recently returned from Ape's World where Maita built and placed a monument to Ape. They went there for the funeral. Ape had died of natural causes at a very advanced age.

Z was feeling lost and alone. He had been very close to the big furry being since they shared the first adventures together with Maita, Thing, Joe and Triss after being abducted from their home worlds by the Pweetoos.

Thing was riding on Z's shoulder, using its empathic talent to relax him. They had a good meal and sat around awhile to discuss old times and stories they remembered with Tab and TR, who hadn't yet been built at the times Ape traveled with Maita.

Iron, Ape's lifemate and Ape's three children and their own

children were each honored and always would be on Ape's World and Vendu.

"Well, Ape lived to see his greatest dreams fulfilled, raise his family and know his grandchildren," Tab said. "He had the adventures with the Emperor of the Maitan Empire and had many friends from several different worlds. Not that many people can have it all! He'll always be remembered and loved by his people."

[He saw us explore much of the galaxy and was with us at first. He lived well and with great value and he dreamed magnificent dreams.]

"That's a beautiful way to say what we all feel," Z agreed. "He lived well and with value. Nothing more can be said for any of us."

We've explored all except galactic south central dome and much between the `S' and `E' beacons. There are only about two billion planets in that area we've missed so far so we should have this little job tied up in approximately one billion years at the rate we're going at present. Shall we begin to plan for our retirements when we finish all that? Ape did all and exactly what he set out to do. I don't think I can hope to accomplish half so much in a relative sense.

"It's strange," Z said. "I'm saddened because Ape is gone, but I'm not depressed or any of that kind of stuff.

"I don't know what I mean. I can't express it."

[He did what he set out to do, then he left us. He would want you to remember his sense of humor and to be able to laugh when you think of him. All of us. I remember right at the first when we took Joe home. I didn't have a sense of humor yet and you two were laughing so hard at Maita's ridiculous movie the two of you dropped on your butts in the dirt and were scaring hell out of me! I thought you'd both gone nuts! I *knew* Maita had!]

What the hell do you mean, ridiculous movie? It wasn't that bad!

"Not that *bad*?!" Z exclaimed. "It was the one most atrocious collections of amateurism it has ever been my horror to witness!"

[I see the humor now. Kicking the sphere out a door open to space? Really, Maita!]

That's just artistic license. It was to explain an action!

"Nobody'd give a license for that!" Z said. "There has to be some content that can be stretched to fit a very open definition of art before there's artistic license."

The special effects were pretty good! After watching those awful things on Earth for decades you have to admit that!

"I didn't watch that crap!" Z protested. "I'll admit yours were as good, but that's no recommendation for anything. The ones on Earth stunk!"

[Yeah, Maita! Yours were as good as the worst every produced anywhere!]

This would go on for hours.

C. D. Moulton's works are available on most major outlets as printed or e-books. CD writes the CD Grimes, PI, mysteries, the Det. Lt. Nick Storie mysteries, the Clint Faraday mysteries, the Flight of the Maita science fiction series, books on orchid culture and many others of many types. Mystery, adventure, intrigue, science fiction, humor, fantasy, paranormal, mild erotica, and factual.